Russia had suddenly become real, a place of substance so real that you could put the tonnage of the *Eagle* down on it. Russia had always been the target, a set of maps and a dim, watery flyover or satellite pictures that experts said showed a runway, a railway yard, a missile installation. Russia was a set of headlines in the newspaper, a word said by all-knowing TV anchormen. Russia wasn't a *place*. It was a factual abstract of the enemy. So if all this was true, what were his flight boots doing sinking a couple of inches into the squashy ground that any map in the world would say was Russian?

"Russia," said Milligan. "Great. I have a feeling we aren't going to be popular. What with us having just nuked the place. . . ."

BROKEN EAGLE

ROBERT TINE

PINNACLE BOOKS NEW YORK

This novel is a work of fiction. Names, characters, places, and
incidents are either the product of the author's imagination or are
used fictitiously. Any resemblance to actual events or places or
persons, living or dead, is entirely coincidental.

BROKEN EAGLE

Copyright © 1985 by Robert Tine

An original Pinnacle Books edition, published for the first time
anywhere.

First printing/July 1985

ISBN: 0-523-42367-5
Can. ISBN: 0-523-43367-0

Printed in the United States of America

PINNACLE BOOKS, INC.
1430 Broadway
New York, New York 10018

9   8   7   6   5   4   3   2   1

BROKEN EAGLE

ONE

The world had been at war for almost eleven minutes, and the SAC B-52G *Flying Eagle* 209 was on course for its target. As yet, none of the six men on board the ship knew what their target was, but they had received their predesignated flight plan from the control at Mather Air Force Base and were now proceeding west northwest. The continental American land mass was slipping away behind them.

Major James Swanson, commander of the ship, glanced down at the shimmering, jagged California coastline and the snaky gray ribbon of Highway 1 and wondered if they would be there when he got back. If he got back.

When he had allowed himself to think of the next war—the final war—he'd always imagined that it would come in the dark of a winter's night. But it was a warm, bright May morning and the sun was streaming through the plexiglass of the cockpit, turning the tight little space into a cramped, hot greenhouse. That wouldn't last, he knew; they would climb to their cruising altitude soon and the temperature would drop until the heating unit strained to fight off the cold. It was a battle that the low temperature always won.

He glanced idly at his engine pressure ratio gauges and told himself it was just another mission. A mile away on his port side was a sister ship, B-52 911, the *Heartbreaker*, and beyond and below and above were more of them, a score or more. Tons of flying steel, jetting silently toward a foreign nation in order to destroy it.

"Whiskey, Yankee, Kilo, Oscar, this is section four, northwest command unit. The coordinate is niner-niner six-six niner-niner. I say again, niner-niner six-six niner-niner. How do you copy?"

A series of numbers slotted up on the VDT that sat between the pilot and co-pilot.

"Copy that," said Swanson tersely.

"That's a roger. Whiskey, Yankee, Kilo, Oscar, out."

There was nothing in the man's voice to suggest he was concerned that his terse message had set the Eagle on a destructive path greater than any other known in the history of the world. Swanson marveled at the unit commander, and he marveled at himself and the rest of his crew. They were going about their assigned tasks methodically, skillfully, as they had been trained to do, as if this were just another one of the thousand practice flights they had been through in the past. Maybe they were all hoping that was what it was.

"So, where we going, Major?" The voice crackled in Swanson's ear. That was Milligan. The Air Force had told him over and over again that there were differences in rank in their organization and he would do well to respect them. He was a flight sergeant, Major Swanson was a major—and as far as the Air Force was concerned, Flight Sergeant

Milligan didn't speak to a major unless spoken to. But Milligan didn't see things that way.

"Milligan, you won't have heard of it anyway." That was Nastrazzurro. His big complaint about the Air Force was that he couldn't smoke a cigar while inside his plane.

"I heard of Moscow," said Milligan.

The co-pilot looked curiously over at Swanson. His head was sheathed in the flight helmet and his eyes were obscured by the green shade, but Swanson could tell what was in the man's eyes. He too wanted to know their destination.

"Okay," said Swanson, picking up the envelope that lay in his lap, "let's see where we're going."

His heavily gloved hands broke through the tough wire seal on the red pouch and he drew out the black folder. "**EYES ONLY**," screamed the block printing at the top of the page. "**DO NOT OPEN UNLESS AUTHORIZED. IMPROPER** . . ."

He swept open the folder and studied it for a moment. All over the ship he could sense the men listening. Wexler, the electronic warfare officer, or EWO, frozen over his ranging dials, Smith and Nastrazzurro, the navigators, staring unseeing into their radar hoods, and way out in the back with the artillery in the tail, Milligan, the gunner.

Swanson spoke firmly into his mouthpiece. "Good morning, gentlemen. Navigators, please chart course 41/42 AAK 66."

"Roger," growled Nastrazzurro.

They were all thinking the same thing: Now, that didn't tell us a damn thing.

Swanson glanced over to the co-pilot again. His name, Marquez, was stenciled large over the brow of the helmet. They called him the Mad Mexican, although he was from Cuba by way of Miami.

Swanson spoke again. "For the time being all I can tell you is that we are bound for a noncivilian target within our predesignated zone in the Soviet Union."

All over the ship there were sighs of relief. No airman wanted the job of bombing civilians. Military to military, force against force, that was how a war was to be fought.

"Nasty?" Swanson spoke again.

"Sir?" said Nastrazzurro.

"I'm going to need ETAs on target."

"Coming up."

"Wex?"

"Major?"

"Any hostiles?"

"Nothing in range, sir."

"Milligan?"

"Talk to me, Major."

"How does it look out the back?"

"Like we're being followed by the entire USAF, sir."

Swanson looked ahead out into the brilliant morning. He half expected to see the Soviet air armada streaming toward them. He knew that for every missile, every plane the United States of America had put into the air that morning headed for the enemy, the Russians had put its opposite number up, bound for its target on American soil.

Swanson half wished that the two forces would meet somewhere over the ocean and, like the aerial knights of the First World War, fight it out between them—a giant dogfight of nuclear steel. But it was not to be. Since the Second World War, bomber pilots had been called "truck drivers"; you flew the mission, dropped your bombs, and you came home. Somewhere anonymous men would assess the damage you did and decide by how much they were winning the war. The difference was that this time Swanson and his men were flying forth to destroy the world.

"ETA target four hours and thirteen minutes," announced Nastrazzurro's voice.

"I'm in for five. I say four hours sixteen minutes," said Wexler.

"You're on," growled Nastrazzurro.

"Put me down for ten. Four and twenty-two," piped in Milligan.

"Like taking candy from a baby," said Nastrazzurro.

The crew always started a line of betting odds on Nastrazzurro's estimates. Pride and belief in his own skills always made Nastrazzurro take each bet. By the end of each flight he was usually twenty to thirty dollars richer. But sometimes winds shifted or an unpredictable thermal came up over the sea and his times were off. On those occasions he paid up and suffered the merciless teasing of Milligan.

"Any other takers?" asked Nastrazzurro.

Marquez looked over his air and wind-speed indicators. "You can put me down for five and give me four hours fourteen minutes."

"Inside information, huh, Lieutenant? Major, I'm gonna have to ask you to keep your eye on Mr. Marquez. See he doesn't go playing with the throttle."

"He'll never get out of my sight, Nasty."

"Okay, Lieutenant, you're in for five."

Swanson smiled to himself. It was the usual horsing around before the real work began. He wondered if these men could only function if they pretended that a nuclear war was no big deal—or hadn't the horrible truth sank in? Did any of them think there would be any place to spend their winnings when they got back, or did they wager the way they always did—to keep a small piece of sanity in a world gone mad?

TWO

The *Eagle* had climbed up out of range of the Russian fighters circling, sharklike, in the defense sectors along the coast. If a fuel line parted or some delicate, overworked part in one of the *Eagle*'s engines failed to function and the big ship started to lose altitude, the MiG-25s that were there just below them would be on the B-52 like mad dogs on a bear.

Just as they had crossed over the sea to the land, they had seen the graceful arcs of some SAMs floating below them. The range was way off—but that was what the gunnery techs always said. The Russian gunners couldn't fix range for shit.

"ETA target sixteen minutes," droned Nastrazzurro.

"Wex?"

"Major?"

"Stand by to arm."

"Roger."

"We got an ashcan at four o'clock, Major," said Milligan. The gunner, in fact, did very little in the way of shooting. His primary job was lookout for hostile missiles.

"Close?"

"Nawwwwww."

"Twelve minutes to target," said Nastrazzurro, as if he were an elevator operator announcing the floor.

The *Eagle* was locked on to her approach. The big engines were chewing up the thin air, hauling the mass of men and machine toward a few square kilometers of Soviet ground that awaited a few tons of explosive in the B-52s bays that would change the character of that piece of real estate for the next thousand years.

"Eight minutes to target."

Marquez throttled back and glanced out through the screen. Dun-colored ground stretched away to infinity. He wondered how many had died already.

"Smitty, how do things look on the scope?"

" 'S weird, Major. We seem to be alone up here."

"Nothing coming up to intercept?"

"Nope. We took those few SAMs forty or so clicks back, and since then nothing."

"Just like intelligence said," put in Milligan. "They always said their radar sucked. They can't find us."

"Six minutes to target."

"Arm," commanded Swanson. He felt a cold trickle of sweat inside his flight suit. He wondered how the others felt.

The quiet, obsequious beeping of the ranging computer passed through the intercom like Muzak. The high tones were slow at first, then increased in speed. The mind of the aircraft knew when to discharge its deadly eggs; then EWO put the information in, the computer did the rest. The tones were coming fast now, like the heartbeats of the crew.

"Twenty seconds," said Nastrazzurro. Even his voice, usually so steady, was tight and dry.

The Eagle rocked slightly as it lost seven tons of weight. The firing-computer beep elongated into a long whining scream.

Cold air flooded through the aircraft as the chilled air of the Russian morning rushed in through the bomb-bay doors.

"We're clean."

"Take her to port, Marquez," ordered Swanson.

The throttles were pushed forward, grabbing for more power. The big ship veered sharply to the left. This was going to be the hardest part of the mission: getting the lumbering aircraft out of the blast.

"Holeeeeee shit!" screamed Milligan into his open mike. "Holeeeeeee shiiiiiit!" He was the only member of the crew that could see the blast. Suddenly all those words he had heard about the devastating action of the bomb made sense. Sure, he had seen the films, but no movie could capture the flash, the blast, the smoke that climbed over itself like a dreadful jungle creeper.

"Wait for the shock," ordered Swanson.

Almost as he spoke the words the *Eagle* was seized by a great wave of turbulent air. It was as if a giant hand had swept down out of the heavens to toss the toy aircraft around and around in the whirlpool of the bomb shock that the craft had unleashed on the innocent ground.

The ship rattled and shook and for a second there was no response on the controls, the altimeter lost its grip on reality, needles danced and jumped. Then the nuclear wind swept on, leaving the *Eagle* shaken but secure on the heavy stream of smooth air that followed the shock wave. It was like suddenly shifting from a dirt track to smooth blacktop.

"Nasty, course."

"We're off by zero zero one."

"Correct it."

"Roger that."

"Smitty, gimme a road map for Guam."

"Roger."

"Milligan?"

For once Milligan was silent.

"Milligan?"

"Yeah?" His voice was sober, husky, tired.

"Bad?"

"Looks like the end of the world, Major."

The crew was listening as Milligan's voice, heavy with emotion, crackled in their ears. "It's gonna make a pretty big dent down there."

The EWO's voice broke in. His equipment was staring down into the smoke and fire that they had caused; the eye in the sky was looking dispassionately at the flaming earth, its mechanical brain piecing the last few minutes of history together to form a picture of the damage done.

"I'm getting about eighty percent," said Wexler quietly. "It's only a prelim and there's so much going on down there that the report could be way off, but it looks like seventy-eighty percent. . . ."

Back at Mather the mission had already been measured a success. But the men of the *Eagle* were suddenly not so sure. Milligan had seen it and the rest of them could imagine it. The same thing was happening on the other side as the Russians realized what they had done to America. Russian computers were looking over Nastrazzurro's New Jersey, Wexler's Idaho, Marquez's Miami, Smith's Chicago, Milligan's Boston, Swanson's Virginia, and dispassionately reporting seventy, eighty, ninety percent destruction.

They had come about and were making south southeast for Guam. Their speed was greater now, as they were light of their bombs and their tons of fuel was dwindling.

Nastrazzurro had read off his estimate, but there had been no wagering this time.

The crew of the *Eagle* had gone numb as the awful reality of their mission sunk in. They flew their craft with precision, with skill, the way they always had, but now it was just a wearying job in the cold, cramped cabin. They wanted to go home. If there was still a home to go to.

Then things changed and changed quickly. Like a chorus, Wexler, Nasty, and Smith started speaking at once. They had been the first to see them. On their scopes they saw a hazardous avenue of death laid out along their flight path.

"We got hostile action," said Smith.

"Four eight, no, sixteen SAMs," broke in Wexler.

"I got one casualty," said Nasty. "It's a BUFF. She's a kill."

Every man on the craft wondered who. There was a B-52, a Big, Ugly, Fat Fucker, going down. Was it the *Heartbreaker*? The *Silver Ghost*? The *Devil Dog*?

The war in the air suddenly became Wexler's responsibility. It was he who took over the job of keeping the *Eagle* afloat. He monitored the electronic countermeasures equipment. It detected the threat, and then its microcomputer mind jammed and jolted, throwing out a dozen different conflicting signals to the onrushing missiles. Wexler bent tight over his equipment. The rest of the crew could only hope that his mind and the electronic brain could outsmart the Russian gunners and the enemy's own intricate computers.

"Uplink," said Wexler. The ALR 46 and ALR 20s hummed with life. Missiles started exploding exactly where their sensitive equipment told them the *Eagle* was. But the *Eagle*'s own electronic strategists had whispered in the SAM's ear, Not here, over there. . . .

The electronic game of deceit raged around the fragile

steel skin of the *Eagle*—and the *Eagle* was winning. Then a needle-sized slice of missile cut into the body of the ship and the odds changed dramatically. In itself the tiny fragment of metal could do no real damage besides tear an unsightly hole in the fuselage. But the treacherous steep piece traveled on into the miles and miles of wiring that were packed into the *Eagle*. It came to rest in the nose, where the brains of the ALRs lived. The defenses of the big ship died a quick, painless death.

"Goddammit!" yelled Wexler. He stared at his lifeless equipment.

Swanson and Marquez felt the ship get heavy on their controls. It was up to them now. It was old-fashioned seat-of-the-pants defensive maneuvering time. But you couldn't barnstorm in a BUFF. It couldn't jink, break, or dive. It just flew. SAMs looking like big candles floated by the screen in front of Swanson. Hazy old advice came back to him: if you can keep a SAM moving across your windscreen, it's not going to hit you.

Milligan was chattering into the intercom, calling out that SAMs were floating around him like sharks. The ship slipped to starboard and lost a thousand feet. The sides of the craft were peppered with shot from exploding missiles.

Then they stopped. As if the ship had just flown through a rainstorm, the missiles stopped coming. The EWO picked up the beeping of a dozen or more emergency locator sensors. A couple of B-52s were down, and when their crews ejected, these locators went on automatically.

"MiG," said Wexler quietly.

Then there was a loud crack, followed by involuntary shouts from every man on board, and smoke surged through the cabin.

The altimeter slipped a couple of hundred feet, then a

thousand, then more. Swanson and Marquez battled their controls.

"Hold, hold," whispered Swanson.

The engines screamed with the strain of holding the dying ship aloft. The rotors clawed the air. The four crewmen aft were shouting, looking for the damage, fighting the smoke, scared.

Swanson had lost track of the altitude lost.

Marquez yelled, "If we're going, Major, it's time."

But even in the time it took him to say this, the ship lost more height. Too late to eject.

"We're going down," someone said.

They were. The ground was bigger now, tiny molehills from the vantage point of forty thousand feet became mountains at five; brown rivers the size of thread widened and took on shape and character, revealing the whitecaps of a set of rapids.

Cut the speed. Put her down. Trees, the glittering water of a lake. . . . Open ground rushed up below them. Brakes. No distraction during flap retraction, said a sing-song voice in Swanson's head.

Marquez had vented the fuel. "Hold on," said Swanson calmly. He heard his voice and was surprised at the conversational tone. Can that be me? he thought.

Nothing—no training, no wild piece of imagination had even come close to preparing the six crewmen for the force of the jolt as they hit. The smack of American machine to Soviet earth wrenched them in every muscle of their bodies. Their belts held them tight but could only hold them still so their bodies could absorb every ounce of the weight of impact.

And the noise. It was the noise of force, of power suddenly arrested by the weight of the world. Not one of them would ever forget it. The wail of the engines, the shearing, tearing, screaming sound as a wing split and tore, as the underbelly of the big old ship scraped along the ground. It was as if the air were filled with the sounds of hell, of the furies, of wailing banshees.

Mechanically, without thinking, Marquez and Swanson threw up the brakes and hoped they would do their job; they sliced into the wind, anchors anchored to nothing but the force of the passing air.

Waves of vegetation coursed past and over the windscreen. The speed at which the ground rushed by made it seem unreal to the astonished eyes of pilot and co-pilot, reminding them of those cameras mounted on the front of a racing car that recording the road from the car's point of view. It felt like, it looked like a hundred miles of Russia rushed by them in a second or two.

Then they stopped. Silence. A silence as unnatural as the noise had been. A supernatural quiet, a calm that had no right to exist in a world at war, closed over the dead *Eagle* like a shroud.

"Okay," said Swanson into his mouthpiece, "who's hurt?"

There was no answer. They were all dead except Marquez. He pulled off his helmet and looked over at Swanson. His face was ashen, his eyes wide. He shook his head slowly and exhaled heavily.

"They're all dead," said Swanson.

His training kicked in. It was time to get the hell out of the *Eagle*. He tore off his face mask and helmet.

He heard someone shouting from the aft. Then Swanson realized they weren't all dead. The intercom was dead.

One by one they stumbled out of the craft onto the ground. Tall grass, soft earth. A blue sky. A quiet afternoon.

They were becoming men again. They flopped down onto the ground and stared at each other and at the ruptured, smoking creature they had called the *Eagle*. She was as large and as useless as a dinosaur.

"So," said Milligan, "where the fuck are we?"

THREE

Under the circumstances it was a perfectly appropriate question. Marquez responded first.

"Russia," he said.

Russia. The word burned itself into Swanson's brain. Somehow, until that moment Russia had never been real. It had never had the sort of concrete reality that other places which he had heard of but never visited had for him: China, Australia, Zanzibar. They were real places—but Russia, Russia was something else.

But it wasn't. Russia had suddenly become real, a place of substance so real that you could put the tonnage of the *Eagle* down on it. Russia had always been the target, a set of maps and a dim, watery flyover or satellite pictures that the experts said showed a runway, a railway yard, a missile installation. Russia was a set of headlines in the newspaper, a word said by all-knowing TV anchormen. Russia wasn't a *place*, it was a factual abstract of the enemy. So if all this was true, what were his flight boots doing sinking a couple of inches into the squashy ground that any map in the world would say was Russian?

"Russia," said Milligan. "Great. I have a feeling we aren't going to be popular. What with us having just nuked the place and all."

Milligan spoke as if he had just woken up. Swanson looked at his five men sprawled on the wet grass five hundred yards from the broken, smoking fuselage of the *Eagle*. They looked half asleep. Not even the chill wind that blew up every few seconds could keep them from nodding off. They looked like a bunch of guys settling down to ignore a football game after Thanksgiving dinner.

Secondary shock, he told himself, closing his eyes for a moment. Swanson too felt tired, more exhausted than he could remember having felt before. The long flight, the delayed horror of having dropped a nuclear payload, and then the last ten minutes of the *Eagle*'s flying life had drained him as effectively as a ten-mile run on a hot day.

His body ached, his mind buzzed. It was as if he had poured every ounce of strength he had ever possessed into keeping the big bird in the air and then putting her down as easily as possible. It was as if he had willed the plane to stay aloft and then willed a safe landing—and through will alone it had happened. First he forced his eyes open. Then he forced himself to stand up.

"Okay," he said in an I-am-in-command-here voice heavy with authority. "Snap out of it."

Smith's lolling head was pulled back. Five men opened their eyes and stared at Swanson.

"Okay, we got some things to do. Nasty, you and Arnie see if you can get some kind of fix on where we are.

"Russia," said Milligan sleepily.

Nastrazzurro wearily pulled himself to his feet, then extended his hand to yank Smith upright. "Okay," said the big navigator, "we'll get you a fix. Gotta go back into the plane, though. Need the sextant, maps, compass."

"We're all going back to the plane," said Swanson. "Everybody up. Come on."

Wexler, Marquez, and Milligan stumbled to their feet and looked questioningly at Swanson.

"We're going to need some gear from the ship. Marquez, you break out the survival kits. Milligan, handle the ordnance, Wex, you empty your safe, and I'll take care of mine."

"Gotcha," said Milligan.

The crew of the *Eagle* walked back to the plane. They clambered over the wing that dipped to the earth and stepped inside the stricken aircraft as if for the first time in their lives. There was a sour smell of burned-out electronics and the metallic tang of leftover smoke. The interior of the craft, usually so neat and orderly, looked as if it had been hastily rifled by a thief. The jolt of the landing had ripped equipment free from its moorings and notepads and manuals littered the floor like a fresh fall of snow.

"Nasty, Smitty, get what you need. Wex, empty your safe." The airmen eased their way through the narrow companionways to carry out their orders. "Joe—" Marquez turned. "You and Frank break out the survival gear and the weapons. I'll take care of the forward safe."

"Check, Jamie," said Marquez. "C'mon, Milligan, you heard the man."

Swanson pushed himself forward to the cockpit and the open safe that stood between the pilot and co-pilot seats. Now back in the plane, doing something, James Swanson felt the fatigue draining away; he felt himself pushing through the temporary shock of landing the ship, of coming so close to death. His mind was coming alive, pulling together the facts available to him. A ghost of a plan was forming in his mind.

From the compartment below the flight deck came Wexler's voice.

"So what do we do next, Major?"

"Good question," came Milligan's muffled voice from aft.

Swanson scooped an armful of documents, maps, and code and briefing books from the safe and shook his head to himself.

"They gotta know they brought us down," shouted Nasty.

"Probably recorded a kill," answered Swanson. "This country is fighting a war. They don't have time yet to check each site."

"Fighting a war," bellowed Milligan, "and losing."

"No telling what's going on," said Swanson, leaving the flight deck, his arms full of classified documents. "I'd be willing to bet they aren't looking for us. Not yet."

"So what do we do?" asked Smith like a son taking a particularly thorny problem to his father.

"Got what we need," said Nasty.

Swanson nodded. "Joe? Frank? How you doing?"

"Broken this shit out," said Milligan.

"Outside. Wex?"

"Set."

"Time to make a fire," said Swanson.

They trailed a couple of dozen yards from the *Eagle* and, with some difficulty, started a fire on the damp ground. The plastic binders burned black, sending a filmy smoke into the sky.

The fire increased in strength and rapidly consumed the

papers. "I don't suppose it matters anymore," said Swanson, "but it's procedure, you know."

Swanson's men nodded. That was Swanson all over—procedure by the book—unless *not* going by the book was a smarter plan. They all knew that the moment the *Eagle* had gotten into trouble he should have given the order to eject. That's what the book said. But if he had done that the six of them would have been in six separate parts of Siberia, wondering where they were and what they were going to do. The Russians would have picked them up at their leisure. Unless the elements got them first. So Swanson had taken a risk and ejected the book instead. Each man there knew if they were still alive at the end of this day or the next, it would be because Swanson would make it happen.

Milligan hefted a bundle of paper and plastic envelopes from the weapons locker in his arms. "First order?"

"It's not an order," said Swanson. "It's more of a personal observation."

He looked at his five cohorts. "Nothing very unusual. It's just that I am not much in the mood to be a POW."

"Me neither," said Marquez quickly.

Wexler, Smith, Nasty shook their heads. Milligan was his usual blunt self:

"No. Fuckin'. Way."

Even as Swanson spoke, he knew it was craziness—but he couldn't think of anything else. "Then I say we let Nasty and Smitty figure out where we are and start moving."

"Where to?" asked Wexler.

Milligan supplied the answer. "The U.S.A."

"Good choice," said Marquez.

"So where to?" asked Nasty. "Tell me where you want to go and I'll tell you how far."

Swanson wet his lips and shook his head at the preposterousness of his own plan. "The coast. Remember, the

Aleutians almost touch the Soviet Union. Maybe we can get to the coast. . . . " His voice trailed away. He was suggesting that six American airmen make a long journey through hostile country, steal a boat, and sail home to a country they weren't sure was still there. Madness.

Anthony "Nasty" Nastrazzurro had the ability to see humor in the strangest situations. His eyes smiled brightly as he listened to his commanding officer. "The Aleutians? Coming up. Okay, Mr. Smith from Chicago, let's tell these good people how far to the beautiful Aleutian Islands."

The two navigators spread out their maps on the ground and fell to figuring out their position the old-fashioned way. The sextant, the compass, and the tables did not yield their secrets easily.

"I swore when I got out of nav school I would never do this again," growled Smith.

"Me too," said Nasty. "What time is it?"

"Nine forty-two local," said Swanson, consulting the Rolex on his wrist.

"Huh," said Nasty, factoring that piece of information into the stew of figures. He and Smith consulted for a minute longer and then the chief navigator sat back on his heels.

"Stop me if you've heard this one," he said, "but we are approximately twenty-eight hundred point three three recurring long klicks from the nearest Aleutian. For the lesser brains in this outfit, that is about seventeen hundred miles."

Marquez whistled and shook his head. The other members of the crew looked as if they were about to reenter the state of shock they had so recently left. Swanson felt chilled; it was worse than he thought.

Finally Milligan chuckled. "Twenty bucks says you're two hundred and fifty klicks off."

Nasty pointed at him. "I'll take that bet."

Swanson smiled. These were the men of the *Eagle* that he remembered. "Let's look over the equipment and then get the hell out of here."

The six survival kits were neatly packed in small nylon backpacks, each one weighing ten or so pounds. They were handed round by Milligan.

"Okay," said Swanson, "let's see what we got here." He tore open the Velcro strips that held the top closed and dumped out the contents. A few aluminum cooking pans, almost as tiny as a doll's set, and some packets that looked as if they came from the generic food counter of a supermarket tumbled out onto the ground.

"One rectangular cooking tin," said Swanson.

The others checked their parcels. "Check."

"A round cooking tin."

"Check."

"One pack freeze-dried—beets?"

"I hate beets," said Nasty. "Everybody hates beets."

"I don't," said Milligan.

"Every *normal* person," Nasty corrected himself.

"Coffee, two hundred grams. Dried milk, two hundred grams. Glucose, three hundred grams. Everybody with me?"

They all nodded, except for Nasty. "Beets? I can't believe the USAF issued beets in a survival pack."

"Meat cubes, five hundred grams. Dried oatmeal, five hundred grams. Multivitamins, one container. Water-purification tablets. Morphine. Aspirin. Fishing line and hook. Solid fuel—"

"Beets?"

"Compass. And finally, money." Swanson held up a handful of rubles, small dirty bills in denominations of one, three, and ten. Swanson riffled them through his fingers.

They all had hammers and sickles on them and a crazy scrabble of writing he could not read.

"The band says this pile is worth one hundred bucks. There is also one hundred dollars U.S. and twenty gold pieces. Please do not lose them. The Air Force takes it out of your pay."

"That's a joke, right?" asked Wexler.

The most valuable piece of equipment was found at the bottom of the knapsack. It was a thin thermal blanket designed to catch body warmth and keep it from escaping. It was light and strong and could be folded into a square the size of a pocket handkerchief.

"I am very glad to see those," said Swanson.

" 'S gonna get cold out here," put in Marquez.

"Frank, let's see the weapons."

There was little the big Irishman did not know about guns. He stripped the packing off the six bundles that he found, to his delight, contained Colt Combat Commander automatics with holsters and a couple of clips each.

"Nice," said Milligan, "but old stuff. Tough but they'll break your arm. Better than them little Berettas the Army has now. They're good guns, but lightweight, know what I mean?" Milligan gave the running commentary as he passed them around. There were sounds of metal snapping on metal as actions were checked and clips slid into place.

Milligan was already busy attacking six larger plastic bundles, stripping them open with the enthusiasm of a child unwrapping presents on Christmas morning. Presently he held up a tight little assault rifle.

"Bushmaster," said Milligan. "Anyone train on these?"

The other five shook their heads.

"Good gun. Light. Stainless steel, so don't worry about getting them wet. Two twenty-three doesn't have a lot of stopping power, but it's got a good rate of fire. I guess it's the best we can expect under the circumstances. Not gonna rate much if we run into a bunch of Ivans with Kalashnikovs. Nice of the force to provide bayonets, though."

He passed around the bulky knives that came with their own sheaths. The men of the *Eagle* began stripping off their belts and lacing the knives and holsters for the Colts. He noted that there were only three clips per man, ninety shots apiece. Not much hardware to carry them all the way back to the States.

Each man shouldered his small pack and his gun. Overall, there wasn't much, and the six strong men were hardly weighed down. It seemed like a pathetically small amount of equipment to carry on such a long march. Each man knew that even with careful husbanding they would eventually have to live off the land—and that meant contact with people and that meant danger. But it couldn't be helped.

"Point the way, Nasty," said Swanson.

They walked slowly away from the plane. When they had gone a hundred yards, Milligan cried out, "Holy shit! Almost forgot. Time, everybody." He made the basketball T with his hands and scampered back to the aircraft while his five companions waited, mystified. He returned with something cradled in his arms, something that glinted in the weak rays of the watery sun.

"What the hell is that?" asked Swanson.

Milligan held up a stumpy, thick-barreled shotgun.

"IGA twelve-gauge," he said happily. "Coach gun. Great little weapon." A double belt of cartridges wrapped his big chest in an X, making him look like an Irish version of a Mexican bandidos in an old movie.

"You've been flying with that thing?" demanded Swanson.

"Yessir," said Milligan.

"That's not procedure," said Swanson.

"Maybe not, sir," said Milligan, smiling, "but I always figured that it might come in handy."

"How come?"

Milligan grinned. "Well, Major, I had a feeling we'd all end up in the shit someday."

The four others laughed. Swanson couldn't help grinning. "Okay, Frank. You're right for once."

They walked on. When they had gone a mile, the first of hundreds, Swanson looked back over his shoulder and saw the broken *Eagle* standing out against the sky as big as a barn.

FOUR

An hour after nightfall they stopped. In the various manuals that they had all been required to study in the course of their military education, there had been long chapters devoted to the proper siting and planning of a campsite. Like most soldiers the six men from the *Eagle* had a take-'em-or-leave-'em attitude toward the meticulous guidelines laid down by the authors of training manuals. The long, damp, chilly wind that had slapped their faces and made their eyes stream all day had turned sharply colder and had worked its way through their flight suits. Now each wished that he could recall all that he had read about surviving in the cold.

When they found a slight, saucerlike depression in the ground that could accommodate them all, they took it. They conveniently forgot the USAF's opinions about fields of fire, hygienic placing of latrines, and the establishing of lines of communication. Of course, even the USAF would have forgiven them for ignoring the last. Communicate with whom?

A brackish stream, nothing more than a scratch in the ground, provided enough water for them to boil a couple of dried-meat cubes in a cooking can. They each got three hot, watery mouthfuls, which they finished off with a vitamin pill each.

"Couldn't eat another thing," said Marquez sarcastically. He wrapped himself in his thin but warm thermal blanket.

Milligan hunched forward, his blanket crackling on his shoulders each time he moved. He wore it as an old lady would wear a shawl. He was a big eater. A typical Milligan meal would feed a normal family of four for a week.

Very miserably, he said, "I could."

"We all could," said Swanson, "but you'll only make yourself feel like shit if you think about it."

It was something he remembered from his survival training: if you're hungry, keep your mind off food. Thirsty? Think about anything but water.

Like all the other trainees in the survival course, Swanson had laughed when that piece of information had been imparted to them with all the solemnity of holy writ.

At the time it had seemed so remote and, worse than that, it had seemed trite; what the hell else could you do? Any damn fool could figure out that if you didn't think about what you didn't have, it would make it easier to bear. Swanson remembered the pasty-white face of the civilian psychologist, blinking behind his horn-rims. The man didn't smoke, drank only small amounts of expensive white wine, went to bed early, jogged, and watched his weight, and he looked terrible. His audience was made up of young flight officers who drank whatever they could get their hands on whenever they could. They consumed large quantities of red meat, fried food, and stayed up late picking up women at a dozen honkytonk bars near the base. But they were nut-brown pictures of health, bellies as hard as coiled cable. They were tough enough to absorb a punch from a trucker used to pushing a Peterbilt all over the lower forty-eight and then could deck him with a tap to the jaw.

Swanson could hear the psychologist's Harvard voice. "Organize story-telling sessions among your men. . . ."

Swanson remembered the smiles that shot around the room. The big men looked uncomfortable in their little student chairs, like adults made to sit in a kids' playhouse. They belonged outside or, better yet, in the air, controlling a couple of tons of flying machinery as sensitive as hothouse flowers, as temperamental as an old cat. School was something for someone else. They were young air warriors, men who could sit motionless and still seem to swagger. They plainly thought that the civilian head-shrinker was full of shit. They made no attempt to hide it.

Employing the tactics of servicemen the world over, they spoke to civilians in an exaggeratedly polite manner that highlighted rather than concealed the contempt they felt.

"Perhaps, sir, with respect, you might be able to suggest just what type of tales, story-wise I mean, sir, we might employ," asked Scotty with a perfectly straight face. Scotty had been Swanson's best friend. They met in basic and together they had taken on all the Air Force dished out. Swanson wondered where Scotty was tonight.

Rather than being offended by the question, the civilian welcomed it. "Anything, anything at all. Keep talking. Keep your and their minds off the situation at hand. Jokes, ghost stories, the story of your life. Poetry is good—"

"There was a young girl from Nantucket . . ." shouted a voice from the back of the room, and the twenty-five young men had cracked up. The shrink had looked annoyed. Later, after the lecture he would climb into his Saab and drive off the base anxious to return to what he thought of as his "normal" clients—earnest middle-aged men with a hundred and fifty bucks an hour to spend in order to be reassured that wanting to dress up in their wives' new Halstons was perfectly normal—and swore that when his contract was up he would be done with the Air Force. It had already provided more irritation than it was worth— inevitably at some dinner party or publishing party, someone would say, "Of course, Jason is a cog in the great military machine."

It did no good to explain that he was teaching the young officers about *preserving* life, not destroying it, but his friends couldn't seem to appreciate the difference.

But now, here in the middle of Russia all that the poor misunderstood psychologist had said suddenly made sense to Swanson. Swanson wondered where he was. Probably in a shelter somewhere. Or dead. He would never know that one of his sniggering students had realized that he had made a lot of sense.

Swanson gave himself an order: get them talking.

Nastrazzurro was the obvious candidate. He was funny and gregarious. He and Milligan were already emerging as the two men on whom he could rely. The others were good, tough, smart, but Swanson could tell that the Irishman and the Italian were men with that little bit extra, that inner reserve of strength that they could tap when they needed to.

"Nasty, where'd you say you were from?"

"Union City, New Jersey," came Nastrazzurro's voice from the semidark. They were far north, and it was almost summertime. The dark of the night couldn't quite slam the door on the light of the dying day.

"Italian name, right?"

"That's right. Anthony Guido Nastrazzurro. One hundred percent Italian American from Jersey."

"Yeah," said Smith suddenly, "I always meant to ask you, does your name mean anything? In Italian, I mean."

You could almost see Nastrazzurro's teeth flash in the dark. "Damn right it does," he said, laughing. "Fuckin' right it does."

"What?" demanded Marquez.

"Blue ribbon. *Nastro* is ribbon and *azzurro* is blue. My buddies used to call me on the street: 'Hey, Tony Blueribbon.' "

"Then Nastrazzurro comes out ribbon blue," said Milligan goofily, "not blue ribbon."

"Same thing, asshole."

"Eye-talian," said Milligan. "I used to eat a lot of Italian food. We'd go down the North End in Boston." The way Milligan said it, it came out "nawth."

"Maybe so," said Nasty, "but you ought to try my mama's cooking. That's *real* Italian. Lasagna, veal cutlets, braciola. . . ."

"I could go for some," began Milligan.

Don't let them think about food, Swanson reminded himself. He moved quickly to interrupt the fantasy feast that Milligan was about to tell the crew about.

"Where did you go to school, Nasty?" Swanson figured that was safe. Everybody had a slew of high school stories, most of them funny, that could go on for hours.

"St. Francis de Sales High School for Morons, Juvenile Delinquents, Perverts, Pinheads, and Jerks," said Nasty, "to give it its full name. Run by the brothers of something or other. That's where I went to school, but that's now how I got an education."

"Education? You?" said Wexler.

"Everybody is a smartass, ever noticed that? I'm not

talking about books and history and that kind of shit. I'm talking about life. I didn't learn about life in St. Frankie's, I can tell you that."

"Here we go," taunted Marquez good-naturedly. "Poor boy getting his education in the school of hard knocks, fighting his way up the hard way. Right, Nasty?"

"Hell, no. I learned everything first from the Bombers and then from the fuckin' mob. The friends. Know what I'm saying? The men of respect."

"The Bombers?" asked Swanson to keep the story going.

"The Bombers, man," laughed Nasty, "that was my gang. We were the toughest bunch of little assholes in northern Jersey."

That admission was greeted with the hoots and skeptical laughter that always met claims of toughness from any of the men.

"You?" said Marquez. "You tough?"

"Hey," said Nastrazzurro, "I got busted about twenty-five times before I joined the fuckin' force."

"That doesn't prove you're tough," snorted Smith. "It just means you were dumb."

"I got into a lotta fights. Broke a lotta heads, you know what I mean? Used to beat up on them Hispanic boys pretty good, know what I'm saying, Mr. Marquez? And the Micks— Milligan, you guys—"

"You probably never messed with any cubanos," said Marquez, his voice full of pride.

"I didn't know you were Cuban," said Smith.

"Can you name any other kind of person from Miami? My mom and dad were born in Cuba."

"They left because of what's-his-name?" asked Milligan.

"Castro," supplied Marquez.

"That's the guy. He was some pain in the ass. I learned

about it in school. When I wasn't breaking the heads of dumb Guineas.'' Smith punched Nasty on the arm.

"Hey, Nasty, if you got run in all the time, how did you become an officer in the very particular Strategic Air Command? I thought you couldn't even join the force if you had a record,'' said Milligan.

Nasty laughed. "That's a story and a half.''

"So,'' said Milligan.

"First off I never did any time. Not even juvenile hall. Nothing I ever did was real serious. Youthful high spirits was what my lawyer always called it. You know, fighting, underage drinking, a little shoplifting, steal a car for the fun of it and drive it into New York. Nothing bad, you know, but I was headed that way.''

"What happened?''

"My mother went to the priest.''

"Oh, shit,'' said Wex, "here we go. Spencer Tracy shows up and he tells you that you gotta straighten out and—''

"Nope,'' said Nasty, "not even close. The priest says why don't you get your son committed or disowned? Throw him out. But old Italian ladies don't dump their kids out in the street, even if they were little assholes like Mrs. Nastrazzurro's oldest. So she threw a couple of *maledettos* at the priest and then went and saw Charlie Threesteps.''

"Who?'' asked Swanson.

"Charlie Trescale. He was a local mobster. My big hero. Always had a new Caddy, a tan, always going to the Bahamas. A real big deal.''

"So what did he do for you?''

"Cleaned my fuckin' clock is what he did. Pulled up at my house one morning about eleven o'clock in the morning. I'm just getting up, and then all of a sudden there's this mobster and his fuckin' giant bodyguard, Nunzio, in my bedroom pulling me out of bed, slapping me around, and telling me that I'm a fuckin' disgrace to my dead father— Charlie Threesteps and my dad were old pals—and how can I go worrying my mother this way?"

"So what did you do?" asked Swanson.

Nasty laughed. "Hey, I did what every little jerk who thinks he's hot stuff does. I come up swinging. I went down *not* swinging. Nunzio smacked me and I went out like a light. When I come to, Charlie Threesteps is in the kitchen having coffee with my old lady, talking Italian, laughing like nothing happened. He says, 'Hey, Tony, be a nice boy and get up early and get a job and be nice to your mother or I'll be back.' I said something real clever like, 'Fuck you,' and walked out."

"So what happened?" asked Milligan.

"What do you think? He came back. Next morning. Only this time I'm ready. I have a baseball bat next to my bed. Nunzio grabs it, sticks his fingernails in a crack, and pulls the thing into two pieces. So I'm standing there in my fuckin' skivvies, thinking, 'Oh shit, am I gonna get pounded this time,' and Charlie Trescale says, 'Take a shower and shave real nice and close. We're going for a ride. . . .' Now, in my neighborhood when a man like Charlie Threesteps says we're going for a ride, it only means one thing. It means state troopers are gonna find your body in the trunk of an Oldsmobile on the highway in the Meadowlands, you know? So I think, Holy shit, my own mother has arranged to have Charlie Threesteps take me off her hands. So I go into the bathroom and run the water and open the window, and there's fuckin' Nunzio wagging his finger at me like a nun."

"So what happened?" demanded Smith.

"I shaved, I took a shower, I got dressed, and I go with

Charlie and Nunzio. My mother won't even look at me as we're leaving."

"Jeez," said Milligan.

"And those fuckers put me in the car and start driving toward Newark. Charlie starts talking about the fuckin' Air Force. At one point he takes a Silver Star out of his pocket. Charlie Threesteps, the big mobster, had been in Vietnam, won the double S. Says what a great life it was and how he shoulda stayed in. By the time he's finished, we're parked in front of the recruiting office in Newark. He points at it and says, 'Go in and make your mama proud.' Or what? I wanted to know. 'Or I'm gonna come by and beat your head in every morning until you wise up.' So I joined. I figured it would be easier than having to deal with him for the rest of my natural life."

The five men laughed.

"Hey," protested Nasty, "I'm telling you the force was a hell of a lot easier. He had fixed it with a cop he knew that I had no record. I was born again, a brand-new citizen, no record and a career in the Air Force. He was real proud of me. He used to say that when he died I was gonna be his alibi. He was gonna look God square in the eye and say, 'Yeah, I know I did a lot of bad shit, God, but I made a model citizen out of Tony Blueribbon. That's gotta count for something.' "

"What happened to him?" asked Smith.

"He died. He died in prison. He was an old man by the time they got him. I used to visit him. Even the guards were a little scared of him. . . ."

Nasty's reminiscences had struck a chord. Now the six men mined a rich vein of memories. Every man in the United States Air Force had at least one good story: why I joined up.

Some were simple. "I love airplanes, and what else could

a kid like me do? I was the only kid who joined from my high school who didn't wash out of gunnery school. Makes my mom and dad real proud. One of my brothers is a cop, the other's a doorman at a real swank hotel in Boston. 'Three sons,' my old man says, '*all* in uniform.' Guess which Milligan boy makes the most money. The doorman.''

"Anyone care to guess who makes the least?" asked Marquez.

"Don't have to be a genius to figure that one out," said Wex.

"Yeah," said Nasty, "that's a good point. Hey, Major, are we getting paid for being out here now?"

"Why?" asked Milligan. "If you're not are you planning on quitting?"

"Yeah," said Nasty. "Take a letter. To the Joint Chiefs. Dear Sirs, You don't pay me enough for this shit. . . .''

Smith had always had a reputation in the crew for being the quiet one. He was an excellent navigator, lower in rank than Nastrazzurro, but his equal in skill—perhaps better: more meticulous, better organized—but not blessed with Nasty's seat-of-the-pants instincts. His story of joining up was a little melancholy. He had signed on for a seven-year hitch on the understanding that the Air Force would send him for a doctorate in higher mathematics at the University of Chicago.

"Not smart enough for a fellowship," he said, "not even smart enough to leave it alone. Don't imagine the University of Chicago is standing tonight."

That was a dangerous subject, and Swanson moved to intercept it. Keep their minds off what's going on at home, he thought. They had to keep their minds on the next day's march, tomorrow night's campsite. If they started to look at the big picture, they would lose heart. He had to keep their minds off home. The subjects at hand had already come dangerously close to sentimentality: Mom's cooking, a father's pride in his sons. . . .

Smitty switched tracks suddenly. "Funny my being in Russia."

"I think we all feel that way," said Wexler.

"Well, it's a little weirder for me, farmboy. I *am* Russian in a funny kind of way."

"Now what the hell is that supposed to mean?" asked Milligan.

"My folks are from here. They were born in Russia. I was the first one in my family to be born in the U.S. They emigrated—they say escaped—right after the war. They went to Israel first, then to the States. They are about the biggest boosters the U.S.A. has had since the Revolution. The American Revolution, that is. First thing my dad did with his first paycheck was buy an American flag to hang outside our door on the Fourth of July."

"They went to Israel first? What kinda Jewish name is Smith?" asked Marquez.

"Try Kolonovski on for size. My dad changed it when he got to the States. He wanted to fit in, to be an American. And that's how he thought of himself, but they never did let him join the country club in Oak Park."

"That kind of thing sucks," said Marquez. "Believe me, my family had the same kind of trouble. Then the cubanos took over Miami. Things are different now."

"Hey, it was the same in Boston. 'No Irish need apply.' "

"Yeah, but that was a long time ago," said Wexler.

"Hey, think I could get into The Porcellian Club at Harvard now?"

"Well, if I was you, Milligan," said Nasty, "I'd just concentrate on trying to get into Harvard."

Very slowly, Swanson asked, "Smitty, what language did you speak at home?"

"English, English, English," said Smitty. "My old man was a fanatic about it. But my mother used to speak to us in Russian when he was at work. She used to sing Russian lullabies and tell stories before we went to sleep. When my parents used to have fights, they would have them in Russian. You know, it's a funny thing: no matter all the shit that my mother went through in Russia, I think she always missed it. They say that about Russians, you know. They always miss it, no matter how long they live anywhere else. . . ."

No one paid any attention to that. "You mean you speak Russian?" asked Marquez enthusiastically.

"Now wait a minute . . ." he began.

"You have some knowledge of the language, right?" asked Swanson.

"Hell," said Smith, "I can do better than that. We meet any soldiers of the Red Army, I can tell them one hell of a bedtime story.

"No, c'mon, Smitty," said Nasty, "you can do better than that, right?"

"I can make myself understood, but I could never pass, you know?"

"But you're a hell of a long way ahead of the rest of us."

"I guess," said Smith. "But remember, Russia has sixteen republics and each one has its own language. Look at those ruble notes we got. It says 'ten rubles' in a dozen languages. We could run into someone who's never even heard Russian, you know?"

"Still it's a start," said Swanson.

"I'll do the best I can," said Smith simply.

"That's all any of us can do."

"But I warn you, the way I speak it I might get us into a worse jam than we're in already."

Swanson laughed weakly. "There *is* a worse jam than we're in?"

"You know what I mean."

There was silence for a minute and the six men stared into the dying embers of the fire, each locked into the kind of private thoughts that Swanson had been struggling to have them avoid for the last hour.

Marquez broke the silence.

"How far do you figure we traveled today?" he asked.

It was a question that everybody wanted to know the answer to but no one really wanted to ask. Swanson shifted uncomfortably.

"Oh, I dunno," said Nasty. "Somewhere around sixteen miles. That's about right, isn't it, Smitty?"

"Something like that," murmured Smith.

"Seventeen hundred minus sixteen," began Marquez.

"Leaves one whole hell of a goddamn lot," said Swanson grimly, "but it isn't going to serve us any to dwell on it. We have to work one day at a time. We've done good for day one. Day two will be better. We're a hell of a team. We can make it. The fighting, the running, the living out in the open, that's only part of this. The other part is attitude, morale, keeping our spirits up. We do that and the rest will be— Well, I'm not going to kid you it's going to be easy, but if anybody can make it home it's us."

"Amen," said Milligan.

"That why you been trying to keep our mind off home all night?" asked Nasty with a smile.

"I just can't fool you guys, can I?"

"Nope," said Wexler.

"But I can still issue orders. It's time to get some sleep," said Swanson like a stern father.

The six men shifted on the damp ground, trying to cover

their large bodies with the small blankets. Suddenly the coverings seemed to be about the size of napkins.

Swanson hunkered down, resting his head on a cold, wet patch of what he still couldn't quite believe was enemy territory. In those moments of dark silence, he tried to focus his mind on the next day and what he and his men could do with it. But clear thought evaded all his attempts to grasp it. Exhaustion hit him with the weight of a tractor trailer doing eighty on a stretch of desert blacktop. He slept.

FIVE

They awoke stiff and cold and tired and wet and miserable. Worse than that, it seemed to Swanson that they looked disappointed. It was as if they had gone to sleep the night before secure in the hope that things would be different—better—when they awoke. But nothing had changed.

It seemed as if sleep had done nothing for them physically either. Swanson felt drained, as if the act of sleep were an exertion rather than a rest. He could have sworn that he had closed his eyes in the darkness only a minute or two before. He opened them in the steely light of the new day with the feeling he had not slept at all.

Only Milligan was awake when Swanson blundered back into consciousness. Milligan smiled at his commander.

"Morning, chief," he said, and then added in a burlesque

of an Irish brogue, "And a foin, foin, foin Siba-a-arian marnin' it is too."

"Shaddup, Milligan," mumbled Wexler.

"How do you suppose he knew it was me?" Milligan whispered. "He didn't even open his eyes."

"See any other Irishmen around here?" asked Swanson.

"But that I did, sir, but that I did."

"Get them up, Frank," said Swanson, smiling. "I'll get some water boiled."

They rolled out of their uncomfortable positions, blinking and rubbing their eyes.

"Sleep like a baby anyone?" asked Marquez.

"About as well as a baby would in the middle of Siberia," grumbled Smith.

Nasty jumped to his feet and stretched, trying to work the kinks out of his back.

"Goddamn," he said, "I ache."

He pushed his neck one way and threw his back the other, then rocked on his feet. There was a sound like the cracking of a walnut.

"Ahhh," said Nasty, "that's better." There was another crack. "*Much* better."

Smith looked generally disgusted with himself, his fellows, and the morning. He rubbed his tongue over his furred teeth, a look of dissatisfaction on his face, and said, "Hot shower, Colgate, Listerine, a shot of Right Guard in each pit. Man, I got used to the American way of getting up."

"That, my son," intoned Milligan, "is just what we are fighting for."

Wexler did a few energetic wind sprints to warm himself up. Marquez looked at him bemusedly. "Would you look at this guy?"

"Gotta stay in shape," said Wexler, puffing back and forth.

Marquez laughed halfheartedly. Stay in shape, he thought. What for? To leave a beautiful corpse?

The water that Swanson had placed on the solid-fuel fire came to a boil and he dumped an entire bag of freeze-dried oatmeal into it. It looked wasteful, but Swanson knew it wasn't. He and his men hadn't eaten in—he couldn't quite figure out the number of hours it had been—and they needed something warm and filling inside them. This was going to be a long, long day. A hot breakfast would see them pretty far along it.

They ate quickly and in silence. They spooned each bland mouthful up and savored it as if it were some rare and succulent delicacy. They looked like a bunch of wine connoisseurs, keeping the food in their mouths, unwilling to let it slide into their stomachs. Once that happened, it would be gone.

Milligan cleaned his plate in a matter of minutes.

"You know, I never liked oatmeal until this moment."

"You'll still never get me to eat beets," said Nasty.

"We'll see," said Wex.

"Bet?"

"Sure?"

"Sure I'm sure," said Nasty.

"Twenty-five says that you'll scarf up them beets when they're served, and you'll be grateful."

"Nasty," said Swanson, "I wouldn't take that bet."

"The hell I won't. How come?"

"Because when beet time comes, Mr. Nastrazzurro, you'll eat them because I'm going to order you to."

"The man has a point," said Marquez.

"Okay, bet's off," said Nasty. "But remember, Wex, it was an order."

Nasty and Smith fell to working out their position on the route to be followed that day. It was easier the second day than it had been the first.

"Nothing makes it easier than practice," observed Smith.

"Nothing except a computer," growled Nasty.

The rest of them carefully patrolled the area, trying to eradicate every sign of their ever having been there. It was a routine they would follow day after day. They never knew if it did any good, but they knew it couldn't hurt.

Wexler asked the two navigators a question that hadn't occurred to any of the others.

"What's the name of the island we're headed for?"

"Well," said Smitty, "there are two—Attu and Agattu. Both about on the same parallel and both wonderful places to settle down and raise a family on. Or so I hear."

"Why do you ask, Wex? You know somebody in that neighborhood?" said Nasty with a smile.

"Nope. Just, it's nice to know what we're aiming at."

"I can understand that," said Nasty.

They had packed their gear and the light Bushmasters had been shouldered. The six men were about to set off, but Swanson stopped them.

"Okay," he said, "before we move out there's a couple of things I want to say." Suddenly he felt uncomfortable. The five men looked at him curiously, and it was as if he were facing five hundred strangers. Public speaking was not Swanson's strong suit, and he was also a little embarrassed by what he had to say. He didn't want to give them a death-or-glory, John Wayne kind of talk, but he did want to say *something* to his men. Today the campaign began for real.

He decided to speak his mind. His men had been in the service—had stayed alive—long enough to know heroic bullshit from the real thing. From the truth.

"First off, I don't have to tell you that this mission has about a zero chance for success."

Their tired, haggard faces didn't register any surprise. They had already figured that one out for themselves.

"Aw shit," said Milligan, smiling a smile that seemed to split his face in half. "In that case, I'm going back to bed."

"Shut up, Frank," said Swanson, relieved that Milligan had broken the tension. "But I believe that if it can be done, we are the six men in the whole USAF who can do it."

The men grinned and looked uncomfortable. Praise always embarrassed them.

"We're smart, we're tough, and we're the perfect team. We have navigators"—he nodded toward Smith and Nastrazzurro—"an ordnance expert"—Milligan grinned—"and we even have ourselves a linguist."

"Now just a minute. . . ." said Smitty.

"Shut up, Arnie," growled Nasty, "you're spoiling a beautiful moment."

Swanson ignored the interruption. "But more important than all that, we have something going for us that makes this whole crazy thing a lot easier."

"What's that?" asked Wex.

"Simple," said Swanson, thrusting a hand into his flight-suit pocket. "I figure it's just not in our makeup to become prisoners. We *want* to fight our way home. There's no defeatism here; we want to be free and we want it so bad we're prepared to risk anything to get it."

"*That*," said Marquez, "is a king-sized understatment."

"We just have to remember a couple of things," continued Swanson. "We're men of the Strategic Air Command, and that means we're the best."

"Hell, yeah," said Milligan, all fired up.

"And the best prevail. We were trained and sent on a mission. We accomplished that mission. Now it's our duty to get home." If there is a home, he thought. "And fight again if we have to. Remember our country is at war. That means it's our duty to fight. That's what we've been trained to do, so that's what we do."

"No surrender," whispered Nasty, as if saying a prayer.

"Okay," said Swanson, "end of speech. Let's go."

They marched away in silence, Nasty and Swanson in the lead. Swanson didn't know what effect his simple words had had on his men, and he would have been surprised and delighted to find that his talk had warmed five hearts more than the half pound of oatmeal each had consumed during their dispirited breakfast. Duty, loyalty, a call to arms in defense of their country—these were the sort of things the men of the *Eagle* had been raised to believe in. That made a difference. Each step they took on this enemy land, each mile passed on this barren landscape took them that little bit closer to home, to a country they loved, a little step closer to their duty. That mattered more than full rations and a warm bed with clean sheets. They would never betray the trust that their country had placed in them. They would rather die. It was that simple.

The going was still pretty easy, but Swanson didn't allow them to wear themselves out. They walked for ninety minutes, then rested for ten. They were grateful for the rest but rose uncomplaining when Swanson consulted his watch and announced, "Time's up."

They were strong men, fit and well trained. SAC was not easy duty at all. The day-to-day regimen required that the men serving the Strategic Air Command be up to the strains that constant vigilance put on a man's body and his mind. Any commander of any SAC aircraft, ship, platoon, division, battalion, or army was inclined to think of his men as the best, the toughest, the meanest, and Swanson was no exception—he genuinely thought his five men were the best that the United States Air Force could put in the air. But he recognized that they were human beings, not supermen. They could screw up, talk out of turn, be wrong. They could get tired, dispirited, hungry, pissed off, or downright hopping mad. But they wouldn't lose heart, and that was what counted in the end.

But they were just men. Already, after a single night in the open and with a lot of ground in hostile territory covered, they were beginning to look drawn, gaunt, haggard. Too little food, not enough rest, forced marches, and the nagging worry about what awaited them over the next windswept hill were already beginning to take their toll. Swanson didn't even want to think about what effect private worries about conditions on the home front were having on his men. Whatever they were thinking about, wives, girlfriends, family, it sure wasn't helping them any.

For the most part they walked in silence. The only sounds to be heard were the trudging of boots and the mournful whistle of the wind. As the chilly, monotonous hours passed, Swanson could tell that his men were sinking far into their private thoughts, their minds wandering so far away that they seemed to be in a trance. Swanson himself realized with a start that he hadn't seen the last half mile of territory, had forgotten to call a rest stop. If there had been a Soviet patrol ahead of them, he would have led his men straight into it. For a few hundred yards he was spooked. Not having paid attention to the ground covered, he studied the present path with new intensity, sure that during his trance he had missed something and half expecting a couple of rounds of high-caliber bullets to come stinging out of the gray day, catching them unawares, unprotected.

He shook his head and tried to concentrate, but still his mind wandered. This somnambulant state of mind was so powerful that all they could do was stare dumbly when, about midday, they stumbled upon the road.

"Where do you suppose it goes?" someone asked.

It was a perfectly ordinary dirt road. A country boy like Wex had often walked down a similar road to catch the school bus. The others had seen ones like it from cars speeding along highways.

In this part of the world, however, this would be considered a main road, a cracked and rutted highway with a grassy hump dividing it into two more-or-less equal parts. There was a ditch on either side, but not even the people who dug that ditch believed that it would do what it was supposed to do—prevent the dry dirt road from becoming a muddy trough when the rains came.

Although the crew of the *Eagle* had been in this weird fugitive world for little more than twenty-four hours, the sudden appearance of something so perfectly normal looking stunned them.

The six leaned against the grassy verge that hung over the road and looked at the road suspiciously, as if it were a grizzly they had pumped bullets into but which still might be alive.

Finally, Milligan spoke.

"It's gotta go someplace," he observed.

A few heads nodded.

"No arguing with that," said Swanson. "The question is, do we want to go where it goes?"

They looked down the road and saw that it curved gracefully to the east. The brown stripe lost itself in the wasteland in the distance.

"This thing marked on your maps?" asked Swanson of Smith and Nastrazzurro.

The two navigators unfolded the maps they had been issued by the SAC and studied them closely.

"Well," said Smith, "truth be told, sir, these aren't exactly road maps. There's nothing here showing any road. I think that SAC Intelligence never really figured anyone being in our position before."

"No road," said Nasty simply. He folded his map and slipped it back into the clear plastic case. "Shows the Trans-Siberian Railroad, though."

"And where's that?" asked Marquez.

"Long way away, *muchacho*," said Nasty with a smile.

"If we follow this," asked Swanson, "you have any idea how far it will take us off course?"

Nasty looked at the gently curving road, then pulled out his bulky compass. He stared at it, then looked at the road, then looked at where he thought the sun lurked behind leaden clouds, shrugged, and handed the instrument to Smith.

Smitty looked and thought and then handed it back. They exchanged glances like spies.

"I dunno," said Nasty finally. "I'd guess a degree or two. Not much if you consider the variation involved in the distance we're aiming to travel."

"Just what the hell does that mean?" asked Milligan.

"It means that it's a lot easier to go a little farther and travel it over a road than to go dead reckoning and travel over—"

"Shh," said Swanson, suddenly lowering her head like a pointer. "Listen. . . ."

They listened.

"Listen for what?" whispered Milligan.

"Shush," said Swanson, holding up his hand. "Hear it?"

A silence so thick they could almost touch it settled on the small group of men. They turned one ear into the wind in the hope of catching whatever it was their leader had heard.

On the edge of the wind, fading away, was the low grumble of an engine. The sound shimmered faintly in the air for a second, then receded like the tide going out. Then it was gone.

"Yeah," said Nasty, "I heard it."

"Me too," added Milligan.

"We all did," said Swanson. But now it was gone. He didn't know whether to be relieved or disappointed. If it was a patrol looking for them, then he knew now that they were close. Maybe that patrol was moving on, but there was bound to be another and then another after that. However, had it been a lightly guarded vehicle, a lone car or truck, then Swanson and his men might have been able to seize it and get some *real* mileage under their belts.

"Well," he said, sliding his hands into his pockets, "we know that this road is traveled. The question is, do we want to travel it?"

"Wait," hissed Milligan.

The sound drifted back to them, louder, like suddenly improved radio reception.

"Coming our way," someone said.

"Could be a patrol," said Swanson quickly. "Let's have ourselves a look. Grab some cover. Three to each side of the road. No heroics, got it? I said, got it, Milligan?"

"Read you, sir," said Milligan, diving into the ditch on the far side of the road.

The rest of them followed suit, tumbling into the squashy underbrush and squeezing themselves flat. They had their weapons in hand, ready. From the mushy bracken came the sharp sound of six safeties being clicked off.

The sound was louder now, much louder, loud enough for all of them to realize that whatever was coming was a big, powerful vehicle. They all sent out fervent prayers that they weren't about to come face to face with a SO-122 or a

BMP-1 personnel carrier. Swanson dimly remembered slides he had seen at some briefing or other years before. Try as he might, he couldn't remember the characteristics of each vehicle, but he recalled with chilling accuracy the words of the lecturer. "Get enough of these babies together and, gentlemen . . ." Here the man from Intelligence paused dramatically; he always did at this point in the lecture, and he delivered the lecture a couple of hundred times a year. ". . . only a neutron bomb can stop them."

Swanson remembered looking at his watch and suppressing a yawn. So what? he had thought. This was a problem for the Army. His business was flying, not crawling across the landscape shooting at tanks. How wrong he had been. . . .

He listened closely to the sound. It certainly sounded like a tank, with the low rumbling and that metallic after-clank. And it would be worse if there was an eagle-eyed commander staring out from his perch in the turret. If they were seen, a quick, hot stream of large-caliber bullets would write a quick end to the men of the *Eagle* and their brief, desperate, crazy dash for freedom. Would an anonymous death in the middle of nowhere be better than the humiliation of capture? Swanson thought he knew the answer to that one.

The engines were louder now. Despite the risks, Swanson knew he was going to try and get a look as the vehicle passed. He had to look, he had to get a look at a Russian close up. He hoped that his men didn't have the same impulse. Gingerly, he raised his head from the bracken and peered down the road. He almost smiled at what he saw. Instead of the awesome strength of a couple of tons of Soviet tank, he found himself staring at an ancient Fordson tractor—it was seventy years old if it was a day—towing an iron-wheeled cart behind it.

In an instant Swanson knew what he was going to do.

"Smitty," he whispered, "get that Russian ready."

"Oh, shit," said Smith.

Marquez, on Swanson's left, said, "We gonna take them, Jamie?"

"Yeah," said Swanson. A couple of farmers shouldn't give them any trouble.

The tractor was a few yards off when Swanson stood up, his vicious little gun nestled against the taut muscles of his stomach. Smith and Marquez rose with him. Swanson held up a gloved hand.

"Tell 'em to stop, Smitty."

Smith jumped into the road and shouted in Russian.

The Russian driving and the other perched behind the driver's seat both stared, their jaws dropping just about to the dusty roadbed.

Milligan, on the far side of the road, heard the order and jumped to his feet, Nasty and Wex close behind him.

"He told you to stop, mother fucker," bellowed Milligan, raising his weapon. The look on his face left no doubt in the Russians' minds as to whether he would use it.

The driver stood on the crotchety brakes of the ancient vehicle and the tractor skidded to a halt. With a clang the metal cart coupled to the tractor with a length of chain slammed into the back of the tractor.

"Oow," said a third man appearing from the rear of the cart as he rubbed his head. He was about to say something unpleasant to the driver but caught sight of the six Americans and changed his mind. He said something that sounded to the men of the *Eagle* like the Russian equivalent of "Holy shit."

"I hope you caught that, Smitty," said Nasty, " 'cause I think we're gonna hear it a lot on this trip."

"Tell them to get off," ordered Swanson coldly.

Smith stumbled through a sentence.

The three Russians stood rooted to their places. It wasn't clear whether they simply didn't understand the American or whether they were just too surprised to move.

Milligan advanced a step. "You heard the man," he said. "Get off the fucking tractor." He nudged one of the men in the ribs with his Bushmaster.

The Russians, very slowly and without taking their eyes off Milligan, climbed down from where they were. Once safely on the ground, one of them said something to Smith.

Swanson moved in close. "What's he saying?"

"He's saying that they surrender and please not to kill them."

"Tell them not to worry so much," said Swanson.

Smith translated and the men appeared to relax a little, although they kept on shooting worried glances in Milligan's direction.

"Ask them where they're going."

The man mumbled something and Smith listened attentively, occasionally interrupting to ask the man to speak slower or to repeat himself.

"I think he says that they're headed for a place about seventy clicks down the road. There's a town there, but I can't catch the name."

"That's okay. How big is this place?"

"Not big."

"Any soldiers?"

"He says he doesn't know. He says they haven't heard from the outside world in eight days. They're workers at some kind of mine about thirty kilometers back. They've been sent out to find out what's what."

"Tell them there's been a war and we invaded Russia."

One of the Russians was staring at Milligan with a mixture of awe and fear.

"Don't eyeball me, boy," barked Milligan.

The Russian's eyes snapped forward again.

"Eyeball you?" asked Nasty.

"Heard it on a late movie once," explained Milligan sheepishly.

"Listen," said Swanson, "we have got to make some time. I say we grab this old crate and follow the road a piece. How does that sound?"

"Fine," said Marquez.

"Anyone have a better idea?"

"Nope," said Wexler, speaking for all of them.

"Look in the cart. See if there's anything we can use."

Nasty and Milligan jumped up into the rusty old cart and started rooting around in the boxes and sacks that half filled it.

"Arnie, tell them to lie down. Facedown."

Smith was a little more comfortable with the language now, so he rapped out the orders, trying to sound mean and authoritative. The Russians didn't move until he had repeated his orders, and even then they moved slowly. They creaked down to their knees. One of them whimpered slightly, sure that this meant the end.

"Joe, search them. Arnie, you cover."

Marquez lay his weapon on the metal driver's seat of the tractor and began patting down the prisoners. Their pockets contained the sort of thing that one was likely to find on any man anywhere. A wallet, a blurred photograph of a woman and a child. Small sums of money.

In the wide, deep pocket of the rough cloth jacket the driver wore, Marquez turned up something that he thought might come in handy.

"Bingo. Pay dirt." He held up a map.

Swanson squatted next to Marquez and examined the creased, soiled, crude map. It made little sense to him.

"Arnie, I'll hold a gun on them. You look at this thing."

Smith frowned and shook his head. "It's a pretty basic thing. Without knowing what we're going toward or away from, a road map like this doesn't make a lot of sense. It's also homemade. Possession of maps is a crime, I think, in Russia."

"Get one of them up. Tell him to show us where we are."

Smith selected the man, the driver, who seemed to be the leader of the sorry little band. The man, still facedown, mumbled something into the dirt.

"What did he say?"

"He says that he's not going to help enemies of his country."

Swanson nodded. That would be exactly what he would have said, what most people with any kind of guts would have said. He snapped open the holster on his hip and took out his Colt. He squatted down and pushed the wide barrel into the man's ear. The Russian stiffened.

"Ask him if he knows what I have in my hand."

"He says he does."

"Ask him if he is going to help us."

Even muffled by his ignominious position, the man's voice sounded defiant.

"He says his answer is still the same."

Swanson pulled his gun from the man's head and stepped back. He saw the hair on the back of the man's neck bristle like the fur of an angry dog; his back muscles knit together as if to repel the bullet that he was sure would strike him at any second.

"Tell him that I know he's not afraid of death. But we need the information. Because he has proven that he cannot be intimidated, there is nothing to gain by shooting him."

Smith stumbled in his efforts to keep up with Swanson's words.

"So we shall kill his friends instead."

Swanson's words hit home. One of the Russians screeched and writhed in the dust and yelled something. The patriot shouted back.

"What did he say?" asked Swanson, indicating the Russian having hysterics.

"He said he'd tell us anything we wanted to know. The other guy yelled at him to shut up."

"Pull him up," said Swanson. "I want him to see."

The five men of the *Eagle* looked at Swanson. Nasty and Milligan froze on the tractor cart, not quite able to believe that their commander was about to execute two men in cold blood.

Swanson felt their eyes on him, but he refused to be swayed. He stepped toward the two prone figures and cocked the Colt.

The scrape of metal on metal seemed to fill the bleak day.

Whimpering came from one of the men expecting death from an unseen hand.

The patriot looked away.

"Make him watch," said Swanson, tight-lipped. Marquez grabbed the man's thin hair and swiveled his head back to the scene. The sudden jerk of his head seemed to break the man's resolve.

"I will tell you," he muttered quietly.

"Nasty," said Swanson, wiping sweat off his brow, "get down here and pay attention."

The Russian took the map in his shaking hands and explained as best he could their location, the whereabouts of other towns and mines and roads. Smith carefully relayed this to Nasty, who made notes.

Milligan found that the sacks in the cart contained some evil-smelling phosphate, presumably the product of the mines that employed the men. But in a wooden box he found the men's meager rations—some dirty gray bread, a couple of hunks of cheese, and a very pungent sausage. For dessert he found that the three of them were packing two one-liter bottles of vodka.

"Real food," said Nasty happily.

"Leave them one of the bottles. They look like they could use a drink," said Swanson.

"But there are three of them and six of us," protested Nasty.

"I guess it's just their lucky day," said Swanson. "Wex, you grew up on a farm. Can you drive a tractor?"

"That's what I learned on."

"Then start that thing up and let's get the hell out of here."

"A pleasure," said Wexler.

The six men of the *Eagle* took their places in the cart and Wexler kicked the old tractor into life. A great snort of black smoke palled into the sky.

He wrestled the beast into gear and they moved off. As they pulled away the three Russians watched with pale, impassive eyes. Swanson looked back at the man who refused to cooperate and thought about how a farmer in Kansas, a miner in West Virginia, or a New York cabdriver would have acted if he had suddenly been confronted by six stranded Russians. He wondered if he, Swanson, really would have shot those men. He didn't know. He was glad he hadn't been forced to find out.

SIX

Anatoly Karkov was a lieutenant in the KGB. But, far from being one of those fabled, shadowy men who work at the ornate KGB headquarters in Dzerzhinsky Square in Moscow plotting the downfall of the decadent West, Karkov was more or less an ordinary soldier. Less, if the word of his superiors was to be believed.

He did not look like the popular image of a KGB operative. He had a pleasant, open face, a bright smile, and his hair was movie-star wavy. Neither did he dress like a spy. He wore a uniform because he commanded a platoon of surly soldiers. He lived in a barracks and enjoyed very few of the KGB perks received by his more shadowy brethren who labored in ease, if obscurity, a few thousand miles to the west.

Anatoly Karkov was, more or less, a border guard. He was one of a few hundred officers assigned to one of the

Soviet Union's internal-control sectors. He didn't chase traitors or dissidents or western agents. He policed other Russians, ordinary folk who wouldn't dream of doing the slightest treasonous act. Most of his charges wouldn't even make a joke about old, almost forgotten Soviet leaders, even men like Chernenko, long dead and buried and all but erased from history. Karkov was a hybrid, a cross between a spy, a soldier, and a bureacrat, enjoying none of the privileges of any of those positions. He did his patrols and had a drink and a smoke before going to bed at night. It was a job. Routine. At least, it had been until now.

All hell had broken loose. He didn't quite know what was going on—nobody did—but divisional headquarters, the central office for this bleak and remote sector, had exploded into a frenzy of wild activity. Instructions came chattering in on noisy telex machines; the orders were countermanded, rescinded altogether, then reinstated with even greater urgency. It was all too much for a simple KGB man to keep up with.

Karkov and everybody else guessed what was going on: war. Even those who refused to believe it had trouble explaining the sudden absence of officers above the rank of colonel. Just before the great flap, they had all commandeered cars and helicopters—the vice marshal had an MI-240 all to himself—and vanished. It wasn't hard to imagine that they were all in a hollowed-out mountain somewhere with good vodka and a large number of those big two-kilo tins of caviar, resting up until it was safe for them to come out again.

Did they know—maybe they didn't—that if there had been a war, it had been a short one? Karkov had heard a couple of rumors about definite, devastating strikes by the "bandits"—that meant the U.S.A.—but orders—confusing, but orders nonetheless—still came in from Leningrad and Moscow, so either the Americans had failed to deal a death blow or the war had ended almost as it started. There was nothing on the radio—nothing, not even the mournful music that usually accompanied a catastrophe. Just silence. No television. No newspapers, of course. But who read them anyway? It was said that farther west cities had been evacuated. Karkov didn't know anything about that. He hardly knew what was going on in his own sector.

He also knew very little about the mission he now found himself on. An order, as homeless as an orphan, as unloved as a stray dog, had wandered into the command bunker from the Strategic Rocket Forces. It claimed unequivocally that an invading aircraft had been brought down by the glorious people's etc., etc., more or less in Karkov's sector. Go and find the wreckage. All this was news to Karkov, for as far as he knew officially, the Union of Soviet Socialist Republics was not at war and therefore an invader's aircraft was unlikely to be in his sector. If it was, then it had no business being there, and was therefore a political matter, far above the authority of a lowly lieutenant in the border patrol.

All this he explained to the provisional commander, a major who had never liked Karkov and who deeply resented being left behind when the other, more senior officers cleared out. The major held up his hand.

"This one is for you, Karkov." The evaporation of the senior officers did have its bright side. Assuming these new heady heights of power meant that he was safe in indulging his likes and dislikes without fear of retribution from the top. The major was the top.

Karkov sighed and set about collecting his men. Seven were blind drunk—he hoped they had at least been drinking vodka and had not gotten into the cleaning fluid—and one claimed that he was sick. As the man vomited noisily, steadily, and monotonously for the next four days, Karkov was inclined to believe him.

Maps and rations had been issued, and Karkov gave his NCO some vodka to bribe the issuing clerk at the motor pool to see that they got a relatively sound truck from the limited supply of vehicles that actually worked. Guns and ammunition were drawn and crystals were supplied for the radio. The men drew lots to see who would carry the radio because it was so heavy that the unlucky soul burdened with it had to walk almost bent double. Naturally, the weakest man in the platoon drew the shortest lot. Things like that always happened to the men least able to cope with these adversities, Karkov, who was philosophical by nature, observed to himself.

Karkov sat up front with the driver, and the men sat in the back, passing around some of the vodka that the sergeant had received to bribe the motor clerk. They were pleased to be out of the command center—too many officers around—and they acted, therefore, like a bunch of schoolboys who had unexpectedly received a holiday. Karkov wasn't too bad as officers went and Boris, the sergeant, was unbelievably tolerant—for a sergeant, that is. Of course, the men of Karkov's patrol—recruits from the gray suburbs of Moscow and Leningrad—were required to buy Boris's goodwill with virtually all of their meager pay. In return he went easy on them and allowed them to spend what was left of their pay buying black market vodka from him. No one was sure where he got the liquor from and no one wanted to know. Overall, they figured they were making a good investment. The army gave them so little money anyway that they hardly noticed it, and no amount of money was equal in worth to an NCO's goodwill and a belt of good vodka.

They laughed uproariously every time Feodor lurched to the side of the truck to heave up some gruelly vomit.

That was the first day.

By the afternoon of the second, the vodka was gone and they were lost. Feodor's wretching was not funny anymore. By the morning of the third day, the truck was out of action and nobody would even speak to Feodor.

Boris, the NCO, looked mystified about the mechanical failure of the truck and insisted that all the vodka he had been given had gone to the correct source—but, he averred, surely Comrade Lieutenant was aware that all the motor clerks were thieves, cheats, and probably homosexual into the bargain.

Karkov knew that it would be a mistake to argue any of these points with the sergeant. In addition, he knew it would be a mistake to return to the base (assuming he could find it) without the truck and without locating at least a piece of the enemy aircraft. For a second he toyed with the idea of taking a hunk of the rusting truck back, but he dismissed that as impractical. He couldn't return without something— the major would own his ass forever if he came back empty-handed. No, if he couldn't get the truck back he would have to buy off the wrath of his superiors with wreckage. He posted a guard on the truck. Everybody hoped it would be Feodor, but it wasn't.

"Awaiting further orders, Comrade Lieutenant," said Boris.

It seemed to Karkov that there was a note of sarcasm in his NCO's voice. Karkov cleared his throat and examined his map as if he knew where he was.

"Hmm," he said, and consulted the impossibly long grid reference supplied by the Strategic Rocket Forces.

"Yes," he said finally, "this way."

He strode purposefully away, followed by his men, one of whom was walking like a hunchback because of the weight of the radio, another puking his guts out. The lone man sitting in the cab of the truck watched them go and wondered if he would ever see them again.

No one was more surprised than Karkov when Boris nudged him in a most insolent manner and pointed to the broken *Eagle* resting on the horizon as big as a mountain. They had been walking for hours, covering mile upon mile, and not once—despite their frequent study of the map—had Karkov had the slightest notion of where he was. He wondered how far away and in which direction the truck was. Then, as he looked at the *Eagle*, another thought struck him.

"Take cover!" shouted Lieutenant Karkov.

The squad flopped down into the foliage, the radio operator getting there first, as he was closest. They lay there unmoving, waiting for the next command. Karkov raised his head and looked at the plane. It was still and silent. If they had been seen approaching, they could be walking into an ambush. Karkov sighed in exasperation. He couldn't risk losing the truck *and* the platoon. He had to be very, very careful. He slipped his pistol out of its holster and issued his next order.

"Forward," he said, "and keep yourselves under cover."

The troops advanced, wondering how to reconcile these two seemingly contradictory orders. They adopted the posture of their commander, which seemed to be modeled on that of their radio operator. They crept closer to the plane.

Nothing stirred.

A wide wave of heroism washed over Karkov. He stood upright and shouted as loud as he could, "Forward!"

He darted ahead waving his revolver. His men were right behind him, stumbling after their suddenly fearless leader and messing about with the safeties on their rifles. They tripped over bits of metal, undercarriage, and engine parts, which were littered around the area like a patchy fall of dark hail. They arrived out of breath under the giant bulk of the aircraft. It dwarfed them and made them feel rather silly. Still, not a shot had been fired and the silence that enveloped them was so complete that it seemed that no shots would be fired.

Karkov, hands on hips, looked in awe at the aircraft. Then, aware that he should do something, he shouted, "You are prisoners of the Soviet Union." It seemed a rather puny gesture, given the bulk of the *Eagle*. And he had little in the way of force to back up his order. When some sniggering broke out behind his back, Karkov half hoped that shots would ring out and rid him of the more troublesome members of his platoon.

But there was no answer from within. No sudden appearance of some scared, sheepish-looking foreigners with their hands up. Karkov sighed again. There was nothing else for him to do but to lead his men into the dark, silent interior of the aircraft.

He clambered up onto the wing that dipped down to ground level and motioned his men to follow him. They scrambled up the steep, slick incline and stopped in front of the black hole of the escape hatch. Karkov wracked his brain trying to remember how many men crewed these giant American planes. He decided it was eight or ten—it could hardly be less. Look at the size of it. Even if there were ten men aboard, Karkov reassured himself that he and his force outnumbered the bandits who might be lurking within. But the Americans would know their way around the plane and he, most assuredly, did not.

Gingerly, like a bather testing the water, he stepped into the plane. Electronic gear, smashed beyond repair, was spread across both walls of the fuselage. A mound of circuitry crunched under his foot. It seemed to him that the wrecking of the equipment had been done on purpose. If that was so, the Americans had abandoned the aircraft and they were probably right that minute marching away from the wreck site.

If that was the case, he thought, let them go. He had done his duty and he suddenly felt rather proud of himself. The tight spring of nervousness that had coiled in the pit of his belly relaxed slightly.

He motioned his men forward. "Search the plane thoroughly."

The men of the platoon clumped into the confined spaces, getting in each other's way, the floppy sleeves of their ill-fitting uniforms catching on the jagged edges of the broken equipment and the exposed wiring. They crept around the broken interior of the aircraft as if they were in a chapel or a holy place that had lain undisturbed for centuries until their coming.

Karkov maneuvered his way up to the tiny flight deck and sat down in the pilot's seat. He put his muddy boots up on the control panel and stared out the window at the flat, featureless landscape.

This would definitely mean a feather in his cap. True, the crew of invaders was nowhere to be found, but that could hardly be blamed on him. He had received his orders and acted on them. Acted on them rather creditably, he thought. Not even the major back at division headquarters could fault him for his performance.

Boris thrust his head into the compartment.

"Nobody aboard, Comrade Lieutenant."

"I know that, fool."

Boris stiffened. One little triumph, one moment of bravery, and suddenly they think they are going to win the Order of Lenin. Nothing spoiled officers like success. They were best when they were kept off balance and befuddled.

"Your orders, Comrade Lieutenant."

A rather unwelcome thought suddenly struck Karkov. The American airmen were not in the stricken aircraft, but they could be in the vicinity. His eyes slid nervously to the plexiglass canopy. They could be concealed outside, waiting to pick his men off one by one as they left the plane. It suddenly struck Karkov that the wise thing to do would be to search the area. He wiped a sheen of sweat from his forehead. Karkov had a sudden, vivid image of his entire platoon bottled up inside the plane, being massacred by a bunch of wild, crazy Yankees.

Well, he knew one thing. If men were going to get shot as they crawled through the escape hatch, he, Karkov, had no intention of being the first out. He had done his brave deed for the day. Now Boris, on the other hand, hadn't done anything particularly courageous recently. . . .

"Take some men," barked Karkov. "Search the area."

Karkov sat tensely for a moment while Boris rounded up some of the men and led them outdoors. There was no sudden fusillade of shots, no quick gun battle on the wing of the plane. Presently, Karkov saw Boris and his men nosing around outside the plane. They found nothing save a pile of cold ashes, the remains of Swanson's fire, which had consumed the secret and classified documents.

They searched for an hour and found nothing.

"So," said Karkov, "now we use the radio."

The man carrying the radio stumbled forward and knelt with his back to Karkov. The lieutenant tried with great tenacity to get through to the divisional command. Six hours later, almost weeping with frustration and fatigue, he succeeded in getting through.

All ears were cocked toward the radio as Karkov excitedly gave his report. The duty operator on the other end sounded slightly bored by the report, but he listened and instructed Karkov to stand by. He stood by for another hour, worrying incessantly about the decrease of power in the battery that powered the set and that accounted for much of the weight that nearly broke the weak private's back. Karkov's orders, when he finally received them, were disappointing. He and his men were to stand guard over the plane and await further orders. The operator unceremoniously broke transmission and vanished into the ether.

The men settled down around the big plane and talked quietly among themselves. As night came on, Karkov settled back on the brush and looked into the starry sky. Where, he wondered, were the Americans? Where could they go? Whatever his problems, he was at least in his own country and eventually he would be rescued, perhaps even commended. The Americans were thousands of kilometers from an even remotely safe place.

Boris coughed obsequiously at his elbow. With great pleasure he informed Karkov that their small force had used up almost all of its meager rations.

"Oh, shit," said Karkov.

SEVEN

If some Russian military bureaucrat had been given the order to prepare a manual for the upper ranks of the Red Army detailing the differences between the right kind of officer and the wrong, he could not have done better than to model the wrong kind on Karkov. The absurdly youthful Colonel Denisov, on the other hand, could serve as an excellent model for absolutely the right.

Where Karkov was unkempt, his uniform bulging and flapping in the wrong places, his face imperfectly shaved, his boots always a shade too dull, Denisov looked elegant and deadly in his uniform, be it dress or camouflage. He was always closely, meticulously shaved. His boots were buffed to a high gloss.

Karkov, although given to some moments of bravery, had little of what the staff training colleges called "leadership ability." He was indecisive, worried easily and to excess, and tended toward the incompetence of the ordinary man. He was ruled by his NCO and cowed by his superiors. His duty was something to be gotten out of the way so he could live life a bit.

Denisov made it a point to be brave always. He was born to lead. He treated his men, and particularly his NCOs, with disdain. His attitude toward his superiors was simple: he took his orders and carried them out—but he did not fawn and he held them in no great awe. Duty was his life.

Compared to the hapless Karkov, Denisov was the perfect soldier. But he was a decidedly imperfect human being. He was cold, cruel, ruthless, humorless, without scruples or morals. He would go far.

An Mi-80 attack helicopter delivered Colonel Denisov to one of the fortified bunkers in which senior members of the military and government were weathering the war. He barely acknowledged the salutes of the two sentries on duty on the helipad, walking briskly by them and through a door set in the hardened concrete of the exterior shield of the bunker.

A major met him at the door and escorted him to the elevator that would plummet them deep into the earth.

The major smiled pleasantly. "News from the West is quite good." It was almost but not quite a question.

"Perhaps."

The major decided that he would try a more personal approach. This Denisov was famous for being a man on the move. It would be well for him to make friends with him now and hope that he would remember him when the colonel had climbed to the heady heights predicted for him.

"A good flight, Colonel?" inquired the major solicitously.

"No," said Denisov.

That was the extent of the conversation between the two

men. The elevator stopped with a jolt, the gate was swept aside, and without a look back at the major, Denisov strode out as if he knew exactly where he was going. He was in a narrow corridor jammed with men, all, or almost all, of them officers. They were all wandering around trying to give the impression of having something extremely important to do. On all sides typewriters clacked and telex machines clattered and men hurried to and fro with sheaves of papers. Telephones buzzed and were answered, hurried conversations were conducted mostly in monosyllables, and the receivers were replaced only to have them buzz again. Denisov elbowed his way through the narrow corridor as if through some Middle Eastern bazaar, looking coldly at these men all desperately trying to justify their being at the nice, warm, safe center of things. Karkov didn't blame them. If they were able to get away with cushy jobs, good for them. Some pretty terrible tales were circulating about the decontamination and bomb-disposal units on the outside.

"The general will see you immediately, Comrade Colonel," said the major, trotting at his side. He didn't look Denisov in the eye.

Denisov nodded curtly. Of course, the general would see him. Denisov was a skilled soldier, a busy man, and had been sent to this place by people in the highest echelons of government. Of course, there was another reason the general would see him: the general was his uncle, a fact that had helped Denisov immeasurably over the years.

He was ushered through two anterooms that were filled with more drones and was led directly to the thick steel door that protected the general's inner sanctum.

The general was a distinguished, elderly man. His most noticeable feature was his mane of white hair and the kindly brown eyes of a peasant. He had been something of a fire-eater in his youth and had had what soldiers call "a good war"—the general's was the now almost forgotten war of liberation in Afghanistan. Politicians spoke of him admiringly. "He doesn't play politics," they said, which was a polite way of saying he would do anything they told him to do and that he had no ambitions to take their jobs either by confrontation or intrigue.

The general came out from behind his desk and embraced his nephew warmly. "Sit," he said, "sit."

"Good morning, Uncle Vanya."

"Vodka?"

"Tea."

"Of course." He summoned an orderly—a lieutenant. In the bunker lieutenants became privates and captains corporals. Generals retained their rank.

The tea was brought, but the general preferred the vodka he kept in his desk.

"Your health, Uncle."

"To your success."

Denisov set his glass of tea on the edge of the desk in front of him. He patted his pockets for cigarettes, found one, a Lucky Strike, nicked a match with a thumbnail, lit the cigarette, and inhaled deeply.

"So," he said. His gaze settled on his uncle, conveying that he didn't really have that much time to waste.

"A bad business," said the old man, shaking his head sadly. "What do you know?"

Denisov shrugged. "There was a war. A small one. Less than three percent of the nuclear arsenal was used on both sides. There was a brief land war in Western Germany. It was deadlocked first and then there was a truce. We lost some ground. Our tanks didn't quite perform as expected." Denisov smiled. That was an understatement. They didn't perform at all, a lot of them. Mechanical failures were blamed, but nothing had been confirmed. "Overall, a degree—but not an unmanageable degree—of destruction."

Seven cities had been vaporized in the Soviet Union, untold numbers of military installations had been destroyed. Deaths were approaching the tens of millions. Parts of the earth had been contaminated and made deadly for centuries to come. A radiation cloud had formed in the upper atmosphere and no one knew—or dared to speculate about—what harm it would do. This, to Denisov, was a manageable degree of destruction. The general shook his head sadly, but he refused to let these melancholy thoughts deflect him from the business at hand. In this way uncle and nephew were a lot alike: duty first, last, and always.

"No one won the war," said the general. "No one is even quite sure how it started. The greater battle, however, is about to begin. The battle for the peace, the battle for history. . . ."

Denisov had to stifle a yawn. "Leave it to the politicians. They will tell the historians what to write." He stubbed out the cigarette.

"World War Three seems to have bored you."

Denisov shrugged. "It did. If it had been done properly, it would have been a far more exciting affair. We should not have stopped until the United States of America was nothing more than a memory. A wasteland that people would dimly recall having seen those silly films about. If one is going to fight a war, let us fight it to win."

The general thought of the confidential report about his nephew he had read. The author, identified only by his code number, had praised the young colonel to the skies and cited his "zealotry" as Denisov's most admirable characteristic. The general charitably assumed that the author meant "zealousness." He hoped so. He didn't always trust zealots, blood kin or not.

"Think what you like, but it seems that you will play a role in winning the peace."

"Will I?"

"Yes."

"How?"

The general kicked back in his comfortable desk chair. "An American aircraft has been shot down. The crash site has been found. The plane is relatively intact."

"The crew?"

"Nowhere to be found. They escaped."

"All together?"

"It would seem so. The plane was landed too skillfully for it to have been anything else but a manned landing."

"For the pilot, yes. For the rest of the crew, not necessarily."

The general shook his head. "None of the escape units had been used. They landed the aircraft and made good their escape."

Denisov smiled. "Escape? To where?"

"Who can say? But they have to be found and they have to be taken alive."

"It doesn't seem very difficult," said Denisov. He would never allow the disappointment to show in his voice. But he had assumed that he was summoned here for an important mission. "Why me?"

"There is considerable interest in this affair. . . ." The general didn't have to spell out to whom he was referring.

"So they chose the best young officer they had to carry out orders."

"And why, Uncle, is there such interest in these American fliers?"

The general shrugged. "Surely it is not too difficult to understand. Put yourself in the position of the leadership. They may have started a nuclear war. I'm not saying they did, mind you, I'm just saying they might have. Well, if you *had* been the one to set this whole damn fiasco in motion, you'd hardly want to admit it, would you?"

Denisov smiled and shook his head. This was as close as he had ever heard his uncle come to criticizing his superiors.

"Exactly. And what better distraction than to have a nice band of genuine American war criminals with the blood still fresh on their hands? Something to take people's minds off things, someone to hate. Someone to point a finger at and say, 'Look, there they are. They did it.'"

"More clever reasoning from our leaders," said Denisov, lighting a cigarette. "First they bungle the job and then they expect that people are going to think that six airmen personally directed the war from the American side."

"You can sneer, my boy, but your orders are to find them." As usual, the general's nephew had managed to annoy him. He slapped a thin folder down in front of Denisov. "This is all the information we have at the moment. Yours is a priority mission. Anything you need will be put at your disposal, unless of course you need anything from Kiev, Tsiblis, Volgograd . . ."

Denisov held up his hand. He didn't need to have the names of all seven destroyed cities recited for him.

"I shall report, Comrade General."

"Oh no, my boy. I am not your commander on this, not at all. Quite the contrary. This comes from Dzerzhinsky Square. Do not do this to please me. You have far more important people to impress than your old uncle."

Denisov shrugged. The KGB held no special terror for him. It was a simple mission, no matter how interested the people at the top were. But, given the literally earth-shaking events that were going on around him, the mission's relatively minor status disappointed him.

His uncle seemed to read his mind. "Perhaps you would prefer body retrieval and identification? They are crying out for men. It would be a patriotic and noble act. Of course you would end up glowing in the dark and you'd be dead in six weeks from radiation sickness. We've run out of radiation shields. The factory was in Volgograd, of course. No, not much future in that kind of work, but one day schoolchildren would read about you in their book of Soviet heroes."

"I'll find the airmen, Uncle. Everyone will be pleased."

"Of course you will. Of course they will."

Once outside the general's office Denisov lost no time in evicting the major, the general's aide, from his desk. He called for a cup of tea, lit a cigarette, and started to read the folder he had been given.

There wasn't much. It began with a terse line or two from the Eastern Soviet Strategic Rocket Command announcing that a battery in ——— (the location was blank; it was a secret) had recorded the destruction of a hostile aircraft at 7:21 local time two days before. An updated communiqué gave the approximate location of the downed invader—an estimate later discovered to have been three hundred and twenty kilometers off.

There was a copy in triplicate of the order that had dispatched Karkov, A.I., and his men on their chase. Denisov ran the name Karkov through his mind and drew a blank. A nobody.

The next few leaves of typescript were bureaucratic renderings of Karkov's first and subsequent transmissions. The ghostwriter had smoothed out the at first petulant and then progressively more desperate wording of Karkov's messages. His strident complaints that he and his men were without food, water, rough-weather gear, or transport was conveniently excised from his reports. It was for his own good. It was better that his superiors thought that Karkov, A.I., was stoically and efficiently doing his duty. They did not want to know that he was cold, wet, hungry, exhausted, and managing only barely to control a group of armed men now almost openly mutinous.

Denisov was more interested in the number that was displayed by the *Eagle*. He summoned the major.

"Has this flight number been checked against the order of battle of the U.S. Strategic Air Command?"

The major blanched. "Comrade Colonel . . ."

"Yes or no? Has it?"

"No, Comrade Colonel."

"See to it."

"Comrade Colonel, the lines to the central computer in the Surpreme Command—"

"This information has the highest priority. You have the authority, Major. Use it."

"Yes, Comrade Colonel." The major sighed. This would mean hours on the telephone.

"I wish to know everything about this aircraft. Who commanded it. Who crewed it. The base it took off from. The target it was bound for. Everything." Denisov spoke in a very quiet, soft voice. He found that he almost never had to shout to make himself obeyed instantly.

"Yes, Comrade Colonel."

"And I want a helicopter. I am going to the crash site."

"Immediately, Comrade Colonel."

"This information will be on my desk on my return." The major did not point out that it was *his* desk. Denisov's first rule of making men respond to your command was really very simple: make them fear you.

Karkov's men did not fear him, although with the passing of each hour he came to fear them a little more. His brief and now it seemed rather cheap burst of heroism when they had spotted the plane had long since been forgotten. His men were hungry and they were sure they had totally slipped out of the memory of the great Soviet military machine. Karkov was not sure they weren't right, but he could hardly agree with them. It would be unofficerlike.

The wind was cold and the air was damp. Shortly after his report of his finding the *Eagle*, thinking that it would be only a matter of hours before relief arrived, Karkov had forbidden his men to shelter within the aircraft itself. Now as it got colder, it would have been prudent to make use of the hulk to fight the effects of the exposure they were likely to die of if they weren't rescued soon. Though Karkov would dearly have liked to get snug in the plane and though he sorely regretted having given the order in the first place, he felt that he would lose all control over the men if he countermanded the order. So they all sat in the lee of the plane, cold, alone, hungry, and, it seemed, forgotten.

The men blamed Karkov for all of this.

He dimly remembered having been subjected to a talk about survival in the wild early in his days in the border-security service. There was something in it, he recalled, about making soup from some sort of green plant. That plus a lecture on avoiding heatstroke—hardly applicable here—was all he recalled. He pushed the thought of eating the shrubbery out of his mind and, like his men, just waited.

Early in the evening of the third day, they heard the helicopter. They didn't caper about and shout and wave their arms the way castaways are supposed to do. They just sighed heavily and muttered, "At last."

Karkov was arguably the most relieved of the lot. He would not have put it past Boris to kill him and desert. But now the frightening vigil was over. At last.

The Mi-80 came out of the low cloud cover like a great mythic bird, swooped over the *Eagle* as if it recognized a member of the same species, and then with a great spinning up of debris and scrub settled a hundred yards from the site and Karkov's sorry band.

Taking control of himself, Karkov summoned up the last reserves of the professional military man his broken soul could muster and started shouting orders.

"Sergeant!" he bellowed in his best parade-ground voice, "get these men in order. At the double!"

Boris, no fool, saw the Mi-80 and with that peculiar, almost druidical skill of soothsaying that experienced NCOs possess, divined that there was a very important person aboard. Up to that moment Boris had subtly sided with the more numerous faction in the war of nerves between Karkov and his men. Now, just as subtly, with the arrival of the real military he changed sides and became Karkov's staunch supporter.

He fell to belaboring the men, screaming at them and swearing, whipping them into a creditable semblance of military order.

Karkov hurried to the helicopter and met Denisov striding across the gorse toward the *Eagle*. He lacked Boris's insight and assumed that the officer sent to relieve him would be of the same rank. He was just about to start berating him for his tardiness and an extremely colorful sentence was forming on his lips when he saw Denisov's colonel's insignia. He gulped and halted, rigidly at attention. Quivering like a spring in his stiff posture, he saluted with a snap, his eyes fixed on some undetermined point in the middle distance. This was accepted military procedure—but he also didn't dare to look at Denisov for fear that the stern-looking colonel would read his mind and know what he had been about to say.

"Lieutenant Karkov, Comrade Colonel, reporting." Karkov watched Denisov glide into and then out of his field of vision. The colonel acknowledged his presence with an offhand flick of the hand. It might have been a salute but it might not have been one either. Karkov decided that it had been and chased after the colonel.

"Very glad you have come, Comrade Colonel," stammered Karkov as if he were welcoming Denisov into his home. "My men . . ."

Denisov had stopped. He planted his feet wide apart and firmly on the ground and looked at the *Eagle*.

"My men . . ." Karkov began again.

"Are the warheads still aboard?"

The color drained out of Karkov's face. It had never occurred to him to check the bomb bay. He and his men might have been sitting on a couple of tons of nuclear weaponry—possibly armed and timed—without realizing it. It was too much. Too much.

"Warheads, Comrade Colonel?"

Denisov looked at him with contempt. "You know, Karkov—bombs."

He knows my name, thought Karkov. That was bad.

"Bombs, Comrade Colonel?"

"It *is* a bomber, Lieutenant."

"Of course, Comrade Colonel."

"And you didn't check?"

There was nothing that Karkov could really say that would make this imperious young colonel more friendly. Well, to hell with him, thought Karkov. He was so angry at the whole damn thing that he considered pulling out his revolver and shooting the bastard. That would be a reaction that this shit wouldn't have considered. But he didn't, of course. He merely stood stiffly to attention and remained silent.

"You are a fool, Lieutenant. Stay here."

"Yes, Comrade Colonel."

Denisov knew that the Strategic Rocket Forces strongly suspected this craft of having bombed a secondary military installation. Therefore the chances of an armed nuclear device being on board were almost nonexistent. In addition, what pilot in his right mind would belly flop a plane with a bomb of any description aboard? But Denisov felt he might as well put the wind up this young lieutenant while he was here. This Karkov was plainly a dolt.

Karkov watched the colonel haul himself into the interior of the aircrat. Karkov was past caring. If there was a bomb on board the plane, so what? If it went off it would vaporize them all in a millisecond or two, with that pain-in-the-ass colonel going first.

Denisov saw immediately that there was no danger. He relaxed and spent a leisurely hour going over the plane, starting at the nose and working all the way back to the tail. Despite his cynicism, he was quite excited at the thought of being inside a flying machine that was the very cutting edge of American military might. He had read that American airmen thought that the B-52 was uncomfortable. After going over the *Eagle*, Denisov was inclined to think that was propaganda, although put out by which side he couldn't fathom. Compared to the Soviet equivalent, the *Eagle* seemed to be luxury itself. Seats were padded and contoured to fit the back of the men sitting in them. There was even a machine for making coffee.

He sucked happily on an extra strong Lifesaver, a half roll of which he had found in Milligan's lair in the rear gun turret. So, he thought, this is America.

He emerged, something approximating a happy smile on his face. Karkov ran over to him. He had had a change of heart while Denisov had been wandering around the *Eagle*. He had decided that he hoped there weren't any bombs on board.

"Everything in order, Comrade Colonel?" he asked hurriedly. What he actually meant was: "Are there any bombs in that thing?"

"Yes," said Denisov shortly. He made toward his helicopter. The pilot, who had never descended from the cockpit of the Mi-80, saw him coming and started the slow warm-up of his engines.

Karkov stared at the machine that was bursting into life. He was a little confused.

"You . . . you're leaving."

Denisov never stopped walking. "Yes. That surprises you?"

"No, sir. It's just that . . ."

"Is there a reason I should stay? Do you not feel adequate to your command, Lieutenant?"

At that moment Karkov did not feel adequate to the task of breathing, but what could he say?

"On the contrary, Comrade Colonel, it's just that the men . . ."

The helicopter engines were screaming now and a great watery wind had been swept up from the slushy ground. It was like being on the deck of a fishing trawler in a squall. This didn't seem to concern Denisov very much. He was well protected in his greatcoat while Karkov was getting soaked.

"The men will do their duty," he shouted.

"Of course, Comrade Colonel, but . . . the plane. What should I . . . I mean what will . . ."

"Lieutenant, I cannot say what the disposition of the capture aircraft is to be. That is not my concern. Rest assured that when the authorities have made up their minds when to tell you what they want you to do, they will make their orders known. Do I make myself clear?"

Karkov wasn't sure, but he knew it wasn't a question.

"Perfectly, Comrade Colonel."

Denisov smiled. "That is what a good soldier would say."

Karkov tried to look proud, but he didn't feel like a good soldier. Furthermore, he wasn't sure he wanted to be one. He would rather be well fed and warm.

Denisov climbed onto the little step that stood before the open hatch of the helicopter. He took Karkov completely off guard by stiffening suddenly and giving him a perfect parade-ground salute.

"Carry on, Comrade Lieutenant," he shouted, his words traveling in a cloud of sweet peppermint. Then he clambered into the helicopter and slammed the hatch behind him.

Karkov dashed out from under the whirling rotors and watched the chopper lift off. Then he turned and faced his men. As he walked toward them, he thought they looked like a pack of wolves.

EIGHT

In four days the six men of the *Eagle* had covered 166 miles. It was a good pace, much better than Swanson could have foreseen, and it had been accomplished with relative ease. Following the information they had received from the reluctant Russian, they had avoided running straight into the town the miners had been heading for. They turned off the main road and continued heading due east on a road that cut off to the right before they reached the town. Since leaving the three men at the side of the road, they had seen no one.

Swanson found himself deluding himself into thinking that maybe, just maybe, they would have a clear shot at the coast, that they might just roll along on this dusty highway without seeing anyone, without firing their guns until they reached the sea. He knew that was a damn foolish thing to even fantasize about. Things could get hard, real hard, in a matter of seconds. They were a long way from home yet.

Wexler drove and the other five ranged themselves as best they could on the tractor and the cart, each one of them taking a section of the horizon. Their eyes were ready to lock on to buildings, people, dust; their eyes swept the sky, scanning for choppers or vapor trails, but they saw nothing. Swanson's optimistic thoughts, no matter how crazy, seemed to have some foundation in reality.

During the short nights, he would dream that they were the last people alive on earth. He saw nothing during the day to contradict his fevered night dreams. But they *were* a target. Six men bumping down a dusty road on an old tractor would stand out like a sore thumb.

Swanson worried about his men. On the face of things it seemed that they never flagged. They continued to wise-crack, to complain gently about the rations the way fighting men always did. They bitched about the cold and told each other they smelled like shit, but they never expressed anything but confidence that they would make it, all six of them. They talked about the beers they would drink, in which bars, and who would pay for them. They could have been a bunch of guys with "California or Bust" written on the side of their VW camper on a crosscountry drive just for the hell of it.

But they couldn't keep it up all the time. Sometimes Swanson would catch a glimpse of one of their faces when the man didn't know he was being observed. One by one they would get a lost, faraway look in their eyes, and private worries and fears would steal over them. They weren't fools, these men; they knew the odds were long, massively weighted against their making it through the next day, let alone the endless succession of days they would have to live through to see the sea. They would have to remain free in order to gain their freedom—and how likely was that?

The total absence of information was the hardest thing to deal with. They were worried about home perhaps more than they were about themselves. They didn't even know if they were traveling home to a country that still existed.

And Swanson worried about their physical condition. These big men needed thousands of calories a day to stay in peak condition. Suddenly, along with the strain of flight across a hostile country and wakeful nights in the open, they had to deal with a drastically reduced intake of food. The real food they had, the sausage and bread and cheese they had taken from the miners, had been carefully husbanded, but it had been pretty low-grade stuff. The bread was dry and crumbly and the sausage was made more of bread and fillers than meat. But that too had run out. The vodka was gone too, although these guys, who in normal times had an exceptional tolerance for alcohol, found themselves getting drunk on a couple of mouthfuls because their starved blood just sucked it up. Swanson cut back drastically on the vodka. He didn't want hangovers as an added problem.

Swanson knew that more than anything else—failing a letter from home, or better yet a nice C-130 to take them there—his men needed rest, shelter, good food. Things, like the letter or the transport, that he just couldn't provide.

On the morning of the fifth day, things got worse. The rough, growly note of the tractor engine, never a sound that inspired confidence, changed to a rasping death rattle. The exhaust smoke changed from gray to jet black.

Wexler stepped on the brakes and the contraption slid to a halt on the dirt road. He shut down the engine quickly, but the engine continued to race even after the ignition had been turned off. Black smoke poured out from under the dented, coffin-shaped hood.

"Trouble," announced Wex as if he were the only one who had noticed.

The six men climbed down from their perches and looked at the tractor as if they were a bunch of parents suddenly disappointed by a child who had let them down.

"Any guesses?" asked Swanson.

"It's pretty simple," said Wex. "Gasket or piston ring's broken or worn down. If we had the right part and the right tools, we could take it apart and put in a new set. But . . ." Wexler shrugged. He didn't have to spell it out.

"Shit," said Nasty.

"Time to walk, I guess," said Marquez.

"Nothing else we can do," said Swanson.

"Call me a taxi," said Milligan.

No one felt like completing the old joke and saying, "Okay. You're a taxi." It wasn't funny at the best of times.

"Let's lower the profile a little," said Swanson. "Tip the thing over. It'll be harder to see from the air."

The wagon was uncoupled and pushed off the road. The six put their shoulders to the tractor and eased it off the road. They turned it over and the tractor toppled onto its side with a sigh like an old dog settling down in front of a fire. The gray bulk was probably a little harder to see on its side than if it had been standing upright on the road, but not much.

"Think it stands out?" asked Wex.

"Not much," said Nasty, "not much more than a zit on the prom queen's face."

"Nice," said Milligan.

"I just made that up," grinned Nasty. "Folksy, don't you think?"

Much as Swanson hated to lose the mobility that the tractor had provided, he had to admit they were safer off the road. They were sacrificing speed for security. Maybe that was for the better. Only time would tell. They paused while Nasty and Smith went through their calculations.

Milligan kicked at the dusty road and coined a phrase. "More voodoo," he said, gesturing toward the two navigators. From that point on Nasty and Smitty's calculations became known as "voodoo" or, in abbreviated form, "the voo."

The country was beginning to change. The scrubby earth they had come to think of as Russia was giving way to a rough, hilly, wooded landscape with outcroppings of rock giving hints of mountains and conifers to come. The change in terrain was both good news and bad. The flat gray tundra had become as boring as a calm sea. It was getting on everyone's nerves. It was nice to have something new to look at. The changed terrain also provided better cover—and that was the bad news. It could shelter them but it could also provide cover for enemies.

They walked on, talking quietly about nothing in particular. As their boots crashed through the underbrush, something broke through the foliage—something small and brown and furry and fast. The six stopped dead in their tracks. Wexler, the farmboy, identified it.

"Rabbit!"

"Food!" yelled Milligan, unslinging the coach gun.

"Milligan," said Swanson as if he were directing D-Day, "you get on the point. You see a rabbit, you kill it."

"Grease it," urged Nasty.

"But don't blow it to pieces," growled Smith.

The six crept forward, Milligan holding his gun lightly in his hands, ready. The sudden appearance of the rabbit had set them thinking of only one thing: game, food, tender hunks of meat dripping in their own juices as they roasted over a wood fire.

"C'mon, wittle wabbit," hissed Nasty ferociously.

"Sshh," said Wexler.

They stalked their prey for fifty yards without seeing

anything. Then, like a school of porpoises gamboling ahead
of a great ship, a half dozen rabbits broke from the
underbrush in a mad dash for life. Milligan never faltered.
The two barrels of the coach gun cracked, the noise echoing
through the cold air, and two fine, plump Siberian rabbits
did somersaults on the ground. The other four rabbits
bounced off.

"Next time, you furry fuckers," Milligan called after
them.

"Frank, that was some shooting," said Swanson admiringly.

"Just trying to be of help," said Milligan with a grin.

Marquez had retrieved one of the animals and Smith got
the other. The shot from Milligan's gun had hit them both in
the head. The animals bled as if through a sieve.

"Cute," said Marquez, ruffling the soft fur.

"Fuck, yeah," said Nasty. "Let's cook the cute little
shitbirds."

Wexler gutted and skinned the two animals, and a fire
was started in a natural grate formed in the cleft where a
boulder had split apart after a few thousand years of hard
frosts and tough winters. As the spits of sweet, greasy meat
were laid over the fire, Swanson could feel the spirits of his
men rise. Genuine hot meat, a nice belt of real protein. If
they couldn't suddenly be spirited back to Mather AFB,
they would settle for this.

Milligan's two unerring shots, followed by the wisp of
smoke that drifted into the air from the cooking fire, alerted
a thin, bespectacled man named Pyotr Oblomov to the
presence of intruders in what he called "his sector."

It was not, of course, his sector, but apart from his
detachment of Komsomol Pioneers, there was nobody
around to contradict him—at least until now. He was sitting

with his band about a quarter of a mile from the roasting rabbits. He and his detachment were bathing their blistered feet in a snow-fed stream that bubbled down miles from the north.

When the storm clouds of war had gathered the week before, Oblomov and his Pioneers had, by some queer quirk of the ponderous bureaucracy, been among the first to be summoned to the defense of the motherland. The Pioneers had been roused from their homes in and around the grim industrial town of Togliattigrad, where everyone was somehow connected to the mammoth Fiat truck factory. They had been placed on a train and sent to Siberia and told they were to make ready an evacuee receiving center in the east. The twenty-five Komsomol Pioneers were commanded by two men. The first was Oblomov, who when not devoting himself to Komsomol activities, was a schoolteacher, and the other was a foreman in the transmission shop of the truck factory. The latter rarely answered the call to duty—and particularly not at this time, when he heard that his detachment was being sent thousands of miles into the back of beyond for no good reason. No such doubts assailed Oblomov, however. He saw his duty and he did it.

Somehow the detachment from Togliattigrad had passed through the troubled land without being stopped. The day before the war a truck dropped them at the evacuee receiving center and had driven off. Somehow Oblomov had expected something else. Instead of the bustling, well-provisioned complex of buildings suggested by the nononsense initials ERC, he and his Pioneers had found a few acres of old wooden buildings—storage buildings of some sort—that were dusty, cold, unusable, and equipped with very little. There was a detachment of six soldiers who didn't know the Komsomol Pioneers were coming and, once they arrived, could care less.

It should have been obvious to Oblomov that a mistake had been made, that the transfer of the Pioneers and the readying of the ERC had been part of a plan that had been drawn up years before and had been either abandoned or forgotten. But no one had told Oblomov.

The next day came the war. No refugees arrived. The soldiers got drunk and drove away in the only vehicle the camp possessed—a cantankerous army truck. As they bumped away down the road, hooting in drunken laughter at Oblomov's shrieked exhortations that they stay and follow the tenets of the great socialist state, one of the Komsomol Pioneers began to cry. Within five minutes the tears had spread like the plague—even Oblomov's newly appointed second in command was choking back tears, and he was almost sixteen years old.

The Pioneers were boy scouts but Oblomov considered them soldiers in the service of the Soviet Union. They wore uniforms, they had been taught that they had been born solely to serve the state. That they were children made no difference to Oblomov. They were his troops, he was their leader, and, dammit, he was going to lead them.

He stamped out the epidemic of crying with threats and then began a systematic search of the camp. He found, to his delight, some treacherous, rusty bolt-action rifles, enough for any of his Pioneers big enough to carry one, and an impressive-looking if cranky Shpagin submachine gun for himself.

Thus armed, Oblomov organized his unhappy band and led them out of camp on a patrol of "his sector," designed, as he said in the inspirational address he made just before setting out, "to secure this area, to detect and destroy any foreign invaders, or"—and here he cast a beady eye over his charges—"to die for the greater glory of our beloved Soviet Union."

The last point gave rise to a fresh bout of sobbing from some of the younger and less committed of his charges that took ten kilometers of hard marching to quell.

When Oblomov heard the discharge from Milligan's gun, his heart leaped. He secretly hoped that it was a sign of a band of soldiers who would feed and protect them, or maybe it was a group of hunters, local men who could point the way toward civilization. Never did he imagine that his yearned-for foreign invaders were at hand.

The browning rabbit meat spat grease into the fire with a satisfying hiss.

"Can't wait," said Marquez, his eyes devouring the meat as it cooked.

"Could be the end of one problem anyway," said Wexler. "As the country changes, there could be a lot of game out here. Birds, deer—this area isn't much different from northern Minnesota, Montana, you know?"

"I lo-o-ove rabbit," said Nasty.

They all looked at him a little funny. "How many rabbits you eat in Shithole City, New Jersey?" asked Marquez pleasantly.

"Plenty," said Nasty indignantly. "*Coniglio alla cacciatore*. It's an Italian specialty."

"Where'd you catch them? In toxic-waste dumps?" asked Milligan.

"Who declared it Dump on Guineas from Jersey Day?" asked Nasty, genuinely bewildered. "While we're asking questions, where did a big Mick lug from Boston, Mass, learn how to kill rabbits?"

"Hitting a rabbit. Hitting a MiG. The only difference is that one's got fur and the other doesn't."

"Yeah?" challenged Wex. "Seems to me you've shot two more rabbits in your career than you have MiGs. Know what I mean?"

"Quiet," said Swanson in a tone of voice that insisted he be obeyed.

"Hey," protested Milligan, "we're just kidding around. I don't—"

"Milligan, will you shut your fuckin' mouth," whispered Swanson urgently.

"What is it?" whispered Marquez.

Swanson shook his head down toward the slope of the hill. "Heard something. . . ."

The six men sat stock still, sensing the air like deer poised for flight. The only sound was the crackle and spitting of the rabbits over the fire.

"Spread out," hissed Swanson. "Take cover."

Noiselessly, the six men fanned out from around the fire and hid themselves behind rocks or lay flat in dents in the ground where boulders had once rested.

Swanson could feel his heart pounding in his ears. A fine film of sweat formed on the grip of his Bushmaster. Were they about to get involved in a firefight with members of the Red Army or were the interlopers just some hunters attracted by the fire and now already running away after catching a glimpse of their guns and uniforms?

Swanson raised his head from behind the cover of his rock and looked down the slope. As he did, a kid, maybe fourteen years old, walked into the clearing. He gazed at the fire and sniffed the smell of roasting meat. He took a step toward the fire, making as if to steal their lunch.

Poor kid, thought Swanson, he's hungrier than we are.

Before seizing one of the spits of meat, the kid looked around him to make sure he was unobserved. He looked straight into Swanson's eyes. Swanson stared back. He hoped he looked friendly. Very slowly, as if trying to avoid startling a wild animal, Swanson stood upright. As Swanson stood, the child's eyes dropped from Swanson's face to his shoulder. There, bright as a splash of blood on fresh snow, was a patch: the Stars and Stripes.

The kid's eyes got bigger. In those tiny, short seconds, fourteen years' worth of propaganda, of political training, of cartoons of grinning skeletons dressed in the stars and bars dealing indiscriminate death, fourteen years of "know your enemy" kicked in. Later it would dawn on Swanson that an American fourteen-year-old probably didn't even know what the Russian flag looked like.

Swanson was not a frightening man. On the contrary, he had gentle brown eyes, a solid jaw, and an easy grin. Kids liked him. His own children never feared him. The children of his friends were always climbing into his lap and telling him their stories and their secrets. But to that Russian kid he was death.

Swanson could read what was going to happen. He tried in vain to stop it.

"Wait," he said. He pointed at himself. "Friend."

But the kid didn't wait. He turned and tore down the hillside. His lungs inflated like bellows and let out a scream as loud and as strident as an air-raid siren. There came an answering shout. A man's voice.

"Goddamn," shouted Swanson. "Get ready."

"Don't hit the kid," shouted Smith.

The firefight lasted about six minutes. It felt like six months.

As the child ran down the hill screaming to wake the dead, a mental but very vivid picture popped into Oblomov's head. Suddenly he saw himself, Shbagin blazing, storming that rocky rise and slaying untold numbers of the enemy.

He did not hesitate. "Pioneers! Forward!"

The kid who had raised the alarm came down the hill toward him and passed, going at a good clip.

The Pioneers were used to doing Oblomov's bidding in all things and rushed up the hill. Some of them fired shots. One let off both barrels of his shotgun, and the kick from the old brute knocked him on his ass.

All the men of the *Eagle* knew was that someone was shooting at them.

"Here they come!" shouted Smith.

Milligan didn't look, he didn't think. He reacted. And reaction for him meant unswervingly accurate fire. With the first pass of his vicious gun, he took down four of the Pioneers. The others pumped bullets down the slope and the missiles struck flesh.

Oblomov, following his Pioneers up the hill, saw a large number of them fall to the deadly fire that seemed to originate from the air itself. Where was it coming from? And what would he tell the mothers of these children? Suddenly he was frightened. He pitched himself forward, facedown on the ground, the heavy Shbagin pinned under his thin body.

Suddenly the firing stopped. Almost simultaneously the six men caught clear sight of a slain enemy for the first time—a twelve-year-old kid, a rusty World War Two vintage rifle in hand, had fallen into the clearing bleeding from a nasty chest wound.

Swanson felt the color drain out of his face. He went weak in the knees.

"Oh shit, oh shit, oh shit, oh shit, oh shit," howled Milligan. "He's dead. The little fucker's dead. . . ." Milligan had broken from his cover, not caring if a Red Army division was coming up the hill behind the kids.

"Frank!" shouted Wexler, sprinting from his position to stand over Milligan and provide covering fire should the firefight begin again.

The other four dashed by them and stood at the crest of

the hill. Littered on the slope were ten or twelve bodies. All children. All dead. Some wore short pants.

The men of the *Eagle* stared. It was the worst moment of their lives.

"We didn't know," whispered Swanson, as if explaining their actions to an unseen judge. "We didn't know they were kids. . . ."

Suddenly one of the corpses moved. A boy raised his head and whimpered something. Smith had heard it before. It was the same thing the miners had said to him on the road days ago. The kid asked him not to kill him. Smith reassured him as gently as he could.

Smith was interrupted by the crack of a rifle from the treeline.

"Damn!" yelled Swanson. The kid who had been speaking to Smith a moment before spun around and toppled, cut down by a stray bullet from his own side. It had been meant for Smith.

"Jesus Christ!" yelled Nastrazzurro.

"Smitty, tell them to stop shooting. They're kids, for Chrissake." A few shots ripped out of the trees.

Suddenly Oblomov jumped up, aimed the Shbagin as best he could, and let fly. The big bullets tore up gouts of earth and went ridiculously wide of their target.

Then it all made wild, weird, twisted sense to Swanson. It was him, it was that thin guy in the black undertaker's suit. An adult in charge of children with some crazy idea of heroism or beset by a megalomaniac notion that he would lead children into a firefight against six highly trained, well-equipped warriors. A hate so hot and pure pumped through Swanson's veins that he could have fired with his eyes closed and he knew he wouldn't have missed.

"Mine," screamed Swanson savagely, and stitched a rip of bullets across Oblomov's puny, thin, retreating shoulders. The would-be hero toppled to the forest floor in a confused mass of legs and arms. He died in a manner unlike the way he had lived—quietly.

Seeing their leader fall, the few remaining Pioneers threw down their weapons and rushed headlong from the inglorious battlefield. Slowly the six men of the *Eagle* came back to life, struggling to deal with the horror they had just witnessed, that they had participated in. None of them was inclined to follow the fleeing kids. Let them tell the world where they were. The six had other things to worry about.

"Jesus," said Nasty, a catch in his throat.

Numb, Marquez walked from body to body, kneeling next to them, turning them over, feeling for a pulse, listening for a heartbeat. There were no survivors. The six had been trained too well. Every one of the little corpses—there were thirteen of them—showed the mark of a hit to the head, throat, or heart. There were no messy belly wounds, no flesh wounds in the legs or arms. The kids had never had a chance. They had run smack into the concentrated fire like butterflies smashing themselves against the radiator of a speeding car.

"Christ Jesus," whispered Wex, "what have we done?"

Swanson heard his cue and he missed it. He was supposed to say, "Forget it, there was nothing we could do."

But he didn't.

He couldn't say it because they couldn't forget it. Even if each of them made it home to the States, bought a farm, got married, had a pack of kids, retired, and had a bushel basket of grandchildren, each of them would never forget that moment for as long as he lived.

NINE

The dossier on the crew of the *Eagle* had grown somewhat since Denisov had first come on to the case. The major had spent all night on the telephone gathering information, making notes, chasing down pieces of intelligence that were hard to come by in the days of peace. Now that the country was in a complete uproar, they were almost impossible to get. More times than he cared to count, his calls were met with total silence—not grudging, human silence but the vacant nothingness of a call that had been launched into a dead system.

Sometimes there was an earsplitting, high-pitched whine. Or worse, an imperious female voice telling him to hang up immediately.

"Exchanges overloaded," the operators would bark. The major could visualize the luxuriant mustaches that each of these nasty women sported on their thin upper lips.

But he persevered and gradually, like schoolchildren dawdling home, the facts began to come in. A telex machine would suddenly clatter into life and spew out a couple of morsels of information. The vast Red Army Intelligence Center buried in the Urals provided some marvelous details. It was from that source that the major found the two telefax photographs of Swanson and Marquez. They unrolled slowly from the machine and, still wet from the fixer, they were rushed to Denisov.

The young colonel lit his fortieth cigarette of the day and examined the grainy pictures closely. They were not flattering likenesses. Many years out of date, they had been lifted from a base magazine that served an Air Force installation in Utah. Swanson had a few more lines in his face now and had grown out of the youthful buzz cut that the camp commander had favored. Marquez looked happy. His eyes were bright. Not too different from the way he looked now.

Denisov looked at them awhile, then placed them carefully in their respective folders.

Swanson interested him most. Denisov rifled through the file again, going over his facts for the fiftieth time.

James Swanson, Major, USAF. He had been in the service for seventeen years. He was now forty years old. He was married to Samantha West of Atlanta, Georgia. They had been married nineteen years. They had met in college at UCLA. They had three children: Ted (Edward), Jim (James, Jr.), and Emily. The Swanson family owned a dog—no name available.

They owned their home outright, although there was an outstanding mortgage on a beach house they owned some seventy-five miles north of San Francisco. A note appended from the KGB noted that this provided insufficient grounds for financial entrapment. Payments were made on time and the Swansons maintained a healthy bank balance.

Neither was there grounds for a "honey trap." The marriage appeared to be a happy one; no evidence of homosexuality or drug use. The KGB had the last word: "Subject unsuitable for approach." In other words, he would not be a spy of his own accord and the KGB had nothing on him they could use to bully him into becoming one against his will.

"Lucky man," thought Denisov.

But it was Swanson's military record that made Denisov see that he was not dealing with any ordinary man. After he read it, the colonel began to realize that this Swanson might not be so easy to catch after all.

If there was an Air Force award, citation, or medal for efficiency, planning, initiative, or creative thinking, Swanson had won it. He had been seconded to the Army for Ranger training and had passed second in his class. He had been rated excellent in jump school. Somewhere he had found the time to get a Ph.D. in history from his old school, UCLA. His thesis subject was the similarities and dissimilarities between the strategic bombing of the Second World War and the Vietnam conflict.

SHAEF in Belgium had requested that he spend time there lecturing on strategic bombing. After six months SHAEF asked that he be posted there permanently. He had turned down full colonel and stayed at SAC.

That made Denisov think even harder. Here was a man who wanted to serve but wanted to serve in some practical manner. He could have stayed at SHAEF, met the right generals, and then gradually worked his way into the Pentagon. He would undoubtedly have worked his way up through Air Force command. It was not inconceivable that, given time, he might have risen all the way to Joint Chief.

Denisov picked up a stray piece of paper. It was a report on Swanson's request that his flying life be extended. The SAC had decided that he was too old for active B-52 command. A medical report, however, attested to the fact that biologically Swanson's body was six to nine years younger than his chronological age. His flying life was extended, of course, but grudgingly. Swanson's superiors made it clear that they were indulging him. They wanted more valuable things from Major Swanson. It was obvious that he was going to retire after twenty or twenty-five years' service and they wanted what they could get before the inevitable rolled around.

Denisov was always amazed that the Americans made their best men retire so young. True, they couldn't run and jump and fall down in the muck with a bullet in the guts the way a teenager could, but a teenager could excel at that well enough for all concerned. That was the sort of thing young men were good at. Men like Swanson were good at other, more subtle things: like thinking. And leading.

So Swanson had made the decision to be a soldier instead of a military bureaucrat, and for that the USAF would have eventually tossed him out. He'd probably have spent his best years working for Pan Am.

Denisov wondered if Swanson felt better about that.

In spite of himself, Denisov felt that he admired Swanson. And Swanson worried him. This was an American who would not give in. As long as he could think, he could fight. And as long as he could fight, he wouldn't surrender. Denisov was enough of a romantic to consider Swanson a noble, worthy foe. And he was cynical enough to naturally assume that he, Denisov, would win, would prevail and humble this strong, proud man.

Marquez, Joseph, would be another tough customer. He was ten years younger than Swanson and had learned at his mother's knee to hate Russia, to hate communism, to fight with anything he had against it. Even the KGB shied away from him. "Under no circumstances whatsoever is this officer to be approached by field agents." The worry was implicit in the warning. Approach Marquez and he would probably tear the field agent apart with his bare hands.

And who did these men lead? Denisov buzzed his major.

"Comrade Colonel."

"Find out the names and the specifics on the rest of the crew of the *Eagle*."

Denisov did not hear the sigh, but he could imagine it. "Yes, Comrade Colonel."

Denisov let the intercom snap off and went to see his uncle.

"Getting everything you need?" asked the general as if Denisov were a house guest he wished would leave.

"Yes," said Denisov. Then, as an afterthought, he added, "Comrade General." There was a cipher clerk lurking nearby.

"Come into my office," ordered the general.

Obediently, Denisov followed his uncle into his plush chamber.

"Please sit." Denisov sat and felt for his cigarettes.

"It is customary, I believe, for a junior officer to request permission to smoke in the presence of a superior."

"Permission to smoke, Comrade General?" said Denisov in his best staff academy manner.

"No. Denied."

Denisov raised his eyebrows and stopped looking for his cigarettes.

"You don't think this mission of yours is very important, do you?"

"I understand that it is of the highest importance to the

Union of Soviet Socialist Republics, Comrade General. I will carry out my orders to the letter, Comrade General."

"Don't play the tin soldier for me. I know what you're thinking."

"To be honest, Uncle, I think it will be an interesting mission, diverting, challenging—highly trained adults playing a grown-up game of hide and seek using the largest playground on earth. But important? No. Eventually, hungry, hurt, and footsore, these six Americans will be captured."

"They won't surrender."

"Some of them might, but I can predict that two of them will not."

"The commander and co-pilot?"

"Exactly."

"I thought so."

"Of course, they could already be dead," continued Denisov, ignoring the fact that his uncle was reading his cable traffic. "We might find their bones someday. But I think not."

"Not dead," said the general. "Those miners reported them alive three days ago. There's been no report of an engagement since."

"A large country, Uncle. Perhaps the report is slow in coming in."

Suddenly the general's demeanor changed. "You must find them. Think of our own men, perhaps shot down in the mountains of Nebraska. What kind of treatment could they expect from the Americans?"

"There aren't any mountains in Nebraska," Denisov couldn't help saying.

The general was about to explode and remind Denisov that he was his superior officer and that he expected to be treated with the deference that his rank demanded, uncle or not. But before he could speak there was a sharp rap on the door.

"Come in," grunted the general.

The major entered and saluted. "I thought you would want to see these immediately, Comrade General." He handed a piece of paper to the old man and left.

The general studied it and grew pale. Trembling, he passed the communiqué to his nephew. "You see, you see what kind of men we are dealing with? Do you see? Children!"

Denisov read the document.

"Barbarians!" muttered the general.

"Perhaps. It is, however, excellent news. We must see that this incident is well publicized. They will be much easier to find if the whole country hates them."

"The whole country hates them already. They bombed this country."

"The bombings killed too many—" said Denisov.

"What!"

"—for anyone to really hate them. Need I remind you what Stalin said? 'If one man dies it is a tragedy. If a million die it is a statistic.'"

"Get out," said the general.

Denisov saluted perfectly and left.

The general stared at a piece of paper but had no idea what it said. Instead, he heard his nephew's voice saying over and over again, "Excellent!"

TEN

Could anything be as bad as this?

Swanson squirmed on the ground, wrestling with his conscience, his thin space-age blanket crackling as he moved under it. He studied the illuminated dial of his Rolex and registered disgust—scarcely ten minutes had passed since he had last checked the time.

They were posting guards now. The kids were sure to be missed. The fact that they were there in the first place suggested that the area was more inhabited than it looked. Once the whole sickening story of the kids' misguided crusade became known, Swanson figured that the country-side would be alive with armed men looking for them.

Swanson was due to relieve Wexler at midnight. His body craved sleep, but each time he closed his eyes he saw those small corpses sprawled on the grass in the warm sunshine. He wanted to get up and relieve Wex, he wanted to have something to do, even something as tedious as guard duty. At the back of his mind he half hoped that they came tonight, that he would be able to strike out blindly at something that could fight back. To lie quietly in the dark was torture. No. No time in his life would ever be as bad as this one.

The other four men were having their problems too. Usually after a day's forced march they collapsed, ate something, talked until the stars came out, waited while Nasty and Smith worked the voo and fell into a deep, deadening sleep.

That was only natural—but only part of their grave-black sleep was due to fatigue. They were healthy men, men used to hardship, so mere tiredness should not have brought on that deep sleep. It was more than that. It was oblivion. The strain of living through each day was such that at day's end their minds urged them to escape, to exit the real world and retire for a few hours to some safe, calm land, a dream world where they were safe. Where the food was hot and plentiful, where there were clean sheets and soft women. All day their bodies and minds grappled with the problems of staying alive and relatively sane. At night the business of escape was taken over by their brains. Sleep was a narcotic.

But not tonight. They tossed and turned and like soldiers everywhere cursed everything—everything—quietly to themselves. The hardness of the ground, the cold air all got their fair share of curses. Milligan, with his flair for invective, took the soldiers' right of mindless complaint one step farther. At one point the gruff gunner was heard to mutter:

"Fuckin' stars. Too fuckin' bright."

Under normal circumstances, Swanson would have found the remark funny. But these were not normal circumstances.

He fell into a foggy, uneasy sleep populated with kids

dying slowly and in agony in dappled sunlight. He awoke at fifteen minutes before he was due to take over the watch. He felt groggy from his short, restless sleep, but he decided the best thing to do would be to relieve Wex a little early.

Wex was a good soldier. As Swanson made his way toward him in a darkness so thick it seemed he could touch it, he heard a round slide into the chamber of the Bushmaster bull-pup Wex cradled in his arms.

That's my boy, thought Swanson. Trust no one.

Wex knew that Swanson was coming up on relief, but the shape moving through the night so casually could be anyone. Don't trust anyone, don't relax, don't blink. Be ready to shoot until you hear the voice, identify it, weigh its tone and timbre. Try to figure every angle. Maybe it's Swanson, but is there a squad of soldiers behind him, holding a gun on him?

"Chill out, Wex. It's me Swanson."

There was a moment or two of silence and then Swanson heard a sigh of relief from his elecronic warfare officer. As he drew nearer, Wex spoke.

"Oh, yeah? How can I be so sure? Who won the 1937 World Series?"

"No idea," said Swanson.

"Me neither," said Wex. "Hope you brought your blanket. It gets a touch nippy up here."

"Yeah, I got it. Anything to report?"

"Nope. Quiet." The sentry post was at the base of a big rock that thrust out from the hillside like a broken, rotting tooth. If the sentry sat against it, he couldn't be seen or silhouetted against the night sky. The position looked down on a flat, vacant valley.

"We seem to have the whole place to ourselves out here," Wex added.

"I hope that stays true for a while."

Wex stood up and stretched. The blanket crackled as he folded it.

"Long watch," said Swanson.

"Yeah. Watch is always long. Doesn't matter where it is. You know how I pass the time?"

"How?"

"I take a bath. Mentally, I mean. I run the water. Get it good and hot. I shave real carefully. I wash my hair. Just have a good long soak. Sometimes I make a martini and sip it while I'm getting the filth off me. Makes me feel a little better, you know?"

"Come to think of it, you do smell a little better."

Wex laughed. "You think I'm losing my mind, don't you, Jim?"

Wexler tried to keep his tone light, but Swanson could tell that he was worried about his eccentricity.

"Naw. Some guys dream about food or women or a clean, warm rack. You dream about hot water. So what's wrong with that?"

"I was a little worried. This whole thing is weird. I mean sometimes I catch myself thinking that this just isn't happening. Like this isn't Russia and this isn't for real, just some sort of strange exercise that some nut in the Pentagon dreamed up. Then today with those kids . . ."

"I know what you mean. I wish it *was* some strange maneuver."

"But I think about those kids. . . ."

"Don't," said Swanson too quickly. "Try not to."

"It's not easy." Wexler sighed heavily.

"I know that. You have to try or you'll drive yourself nuts."

Wex shouldered his weapon. "Don't worry, I'm not going crazy on you."

"Never thought you were. Try and get some shut-eye."

"I'll do my best," said Wex, fading into the darkness.

Swanson settled himself at the base of the rock, pulled his blanket around him, and sat with the Bushmaster resting across his knees. His mind wandered. In fact, he did everything he told himself he should prevent his men from doing. He thought of home, of food, of his wife, Samantha—always called her Sammy. She loomed suddenly in his mind. All at once, in a mental vision as vivid and remote as a movie, he saw her on the beach at Point Reyes. It was wintertime and she wore a down jacket tight around her shoulders and blue jeans showing her shapely legs to advantage and ankles as thin and supple as those of a racehorse. She was laughing and the wind whipped into her full brown-blond hair. Swanson remembered that day. Was it last winter? The winter before? A century before? A lump formed in his throat. Where was she tonight? He hoped the boys were with her. They would know how to take care of their mother and sister.

At first he wasn't sure he had seen it. He blinked a couple of times and shook his head, convinced that his melancholy thoughts had temporarily affected his vision. But it was still there.

Far off, out in the shallow valley eight—no, ten—sets of headlights were moving away from him like fireflies in the night.

Swanson turned his ear into the wind and caught the tiniest sliver of sound. The low growl of truck engines. It was a convoy, a convoy edging across the landscape. Swanson watched them for what seemed like hours. Finally they disappeared behind a rise.

There was a road down there running east-west, a traveled road, a road used for military purposes. Swanson's first thought was to get his men up and away from there.

But by first light a new plan had formed in his mind.

Nasty awoke first, and Swanson took a few minutes to talk to him while the others slept on. As the watery sun appeared on the eastern horizon, the others awoke cold, hungry, and stiff after another night on the cold ground.

A fire was started and some water was boiled. Swanson crumbled the last of the meat-extract cubes in the panniers. It was a treat. Swanson knew something they didn't—it was going to be a long day and this was as close to a hearty breakfast their rations allowed.

"Listen," said Swanson, kneeling in front of the fire. "I saw something last night. Something that might make a difference."

The five men looked at him quizzically.

"Last night," he continued, "a couple of hours ago, a convoy crossed the valley. It seems there's a road down there, about a mile and a half away I make it. The convoy was headed just the way we want to go."

The men shifted uneasily.

"Now, I checked with Nasty on the voo this morning before you all woke up. We traveled far, but it isn't all that great."

"Shit," said Marquez.

"It's not that bad," said Nasty reassuringly. "We've done something a little over two hundred miles. Smitty and me make it two ten, maybe two twelve."

"A lot of that is the tractor," put in Wex.

"Exactly," said Swanson. "And I think it's time we got ourselves another piece of transport. At the rate we're going, it's going to take us three months' traveling, and you know we're going to slow down."

Each man finished the sentence in his own mind. They were going to slow down as they grew weaker, less able to resist.

"Jump a convoy?" said Smith.

"Not the whole thing," said Swanson, "just a piece of it."

"How do we know there will be another one?"

"We don't," said Swanson. "I think it's worth waiting to see if another passes through. If nothing comes we've lost a day."

They looked from one to another.

"Hell," said Nasty, "what the hell do we have to lose?"

But first they had to do a little work on the road. The object was to get the convoy to slow down or stop, but not to make those riding it suspicious—the conventional road-block had to be ruled out.

Swanson inspected the dirt-and-gravel road and decided what they had to do. The nub end of a boulder stuck out of the packed earth. He hoped that under the ground the rock wasn't too large, just big enough to leave a sizable hole when they dug it out. A couple of hours of grunting from all six of them and they finally managed to dislodge the boulder. They sweated over the staves they had cut from a tree as they levered the big rock out of its deep pocket in the hard road. They staggered under the weight of it and finally managed to roll it into the underbrush next to the road.

What remained was a pothole in the track of the right-hand wheel of any passing vehicle, a hole deep and wide enough for an alert driver to want to take it carefully. It was a foot and a half deep and a good couple of feet across—deep enough to ruin a set of shocks if you took it too fast.

The earth was a different shade where it had clung to the boulder. It was a deeper, richer red than the dusty road, and if a driver thought about it he might figure out that the pothole had not developed by natural means. Swanson was counting on his not thinking about it—he hoped he had enough to think about just getting his truck across it.

They settled, three on each side of the road, and waited. An hour or two into their long vigil a thought struck Swanson, a precaution so obvious, so basic that the fact he hadn't thought of it before—even after the events of the day before—scared him. What had scared that first kid? The stars-and-bars patch on his shoulder. And here was Swanson, all set to sneak into a Soviet convoy with all six of them wearing Old Glory on their shoulders. Not too conspicuous.

I'm getting stupid in my old age, he thought. He peered down the road in both directions. They had the world to themselves.

"Listen," he called out to his men. "I forgot something. . . ."

They helped each other pick the insignia off their flight suits. They stripped off their badges of rank, the SAC emblem, their name tapes, and finally their small palm-sized American flags. They scooped a hole in the bank at the side of the road and tossed in all the flimsy pieces of material—all except the flags.

"I don't think it would hurt any to keep them in your packs," said Swanson. They slipped the insignia into their packs or in their pockets, holding them a moment before stowing them away, as if they were talismans, good-luck charms, symbols of faith and survival.

"Anything else?" asked Marquez with a sad smile.

"Nope," said Swanson. "Let's get back under cover."

A surprisingly warm sun burned off the low ceiling, and as the morning changed to afternoon, Milligan turned over on his back and took the sun on his broad face.

"Milligan," whispered Nasty, "you better not be sleeping."

"Nope. I'm just lying here thinking about a blonde on a

beach wearing nothing but sunglasses. She's stretched out under a palm tree next to a cooler of beer."

"Where are you?"

"I'm in the water swimming," said Milligan, "but I'll be out in a minute."

"This girl," said Wex, "what's her name?"

"Uhh," said Milligan, "let's call her Jennifer."

"Has Jennifer got a friend?"

All day they waited. Dusk began to come down like a fog and Swanson couldn't make up his mind if he had done the right thing or not. If no vehicle passed along the road that night, then they would have wasted a precious piece of time, a precious day of freedom. But was a day of quiet and rest a wasted day? He couldn't make up his mind.

The Sixth Motorized Supply Brigade of the Ninth Military District of the Red Army made up his mind for him. The six men of the *Eagle* heard the convoy long before they saw it. They had a long time to get ready and to get tense.

Swanson counted seven trucks running through the semidark, their headlights stabbing ahead of them. He guessed they were three-tonners, canvas topped, a driver and a soldier in each cab. Looking back into the payload of the first truck as it roared past in a cloud of choking dust, the back lit up by the lights of the second, he saw a dozen or so soldiers, all of them dozing against one another. The second and third were similarly loaded. What if it was nothing but a troop convoy?

What if they grabbed the last vehicle as planned and found themselves staring into the barrels of twelve Kalashnikovs? The answer to that question was dispiritingly simple: they would get killed. And that would be the end of it. But the fourth and fifth were empty of soldiers. There were haphazard collections of crates in place of armed men.

The sixth had more supplies. The seventh had a few crates and a bored, sleepy rear guard. His helmeted head rested on the barrel of his gun as if he were trying to muster up enough courage to shoot himself between the eyes.

A sudden change in the note of the engine from the first truck showed that the driver had seen the hole, hit the brakes, and changed gear. The convoy, like a line of elephants in a circus, slowed down and bunched up. Brake lights gleamed like rubies.

The last truck slowed, then stopped.

This was it.

Swanson led, Milligan on one side, Marquez on the other. The rumbling of idling engines filled the night. The six men moved under cover of the noise, silently and swiftly, six deadly shadows.

The rear guard, awoken by the sudden halt of his truck, lifted his head sleepily off his rifle. Milligan jumped a couple of feet in the air, putting all his weight behind the savage blow he delivered to the rear guard's head. He slammed the heavy butt of the coach gun against the hapless man's jaw. Over the noise of the engines of the convoy, all six of them heard the snap of the sentry's teeth and the gristly tearing sound as his jaw gave way.

Marquez was the next wave of attack. He threw himself headfirst into the rear of the truck, pinned the bleeding and dazed soldier to the deck, holding him down with a knee on each shoulder. A knife blade glittered in the gloom. Marquez flopped off the man as the others swarmed into the rear of the truck like pirates taking over a merchantman.

"All aboard?" whispered Swanson.

"Check," said someone.

Marquez was sure that the beating of his heart could be heard well above the roar of the engines as the convoy began moving again. He had never killed a man close up before. The smell of the man's unwashed body was etched inside his nostrils. When he closed his eyes he could see the dead man's bewildered, scared, bleeding face. He felt shaken and slightly ashamed of himself. But it had to be done.

The six held their breath as their own vehicle began to move, bounced through the pothole, and then picked up speed to join the other members of the convoy.

"What about him?" said Marquez, pointing at the corpse. He didn't like having the body of the man whose life he had taken lying there reminding him of his action.

"We can't throw him out. Another convoy might find him before we get clear."

"What about them?" asked Wexler hoarsely. He gestured toward the front of the truck with his thumb. The driver's compartment was a separate metal shell, unconnected with the payload.

Swanson pushed a hand across the thick stubble on his chin; his brain was busy, figuring the odds.

"We'll have to take care of them eventually. It's just a question of when," said Milligan.

"But we have to figure what we're going to do well in advance," said Smith.

"We can get onto the roof of the cab," said Nasty. "There's a gunner's hatch up there."

"Means shooting," Wexler pointed out.

"And these trucks got them big outrigger mirrors. Any of the other trucks could see us if we took down the driver and his buddy."

Suddenly the whole thing didn't seem like such a great idea to Swanson. Getting into the convoy had been relatively easy. Getting out was going to be a totally different story.

"Okay," said Swanson. "There's not a hell of a lot we can do. It's gonna involve a lot of thinking on our feet. Eventually they're going to stop. When they do, we grab the truck and break out. Maximum confusion. Remember, they are not going to expect to find us sitting in their laps like this. We'll have surprise on our side. All we need is some luck."

It wasn't much of a plan and they all knew it, but it was the best they could hope for at the moment.

"Lesse what we have here," said Nasty, fingering one of the packing cases that surrounded them.

"Let's just be quiet about it," cautioned Swanson.

Nasty slid his bayonet out of his belt and began jimmying the nails that secured the top of the nearest crate. With a creak and the whine of splitting wood, he pried open the chest. He swept back an armful of packing straw. Underneath were row upon row of cardboard boxes, each containing ten vials of pale brown liquid.

"Medicine," said Smith. "Looks like morphine."

Milligan was attacking another box.

"For Chrissake, Frank!" whispered Swanson. He was sure the sound of his opening the boxes could be heard in the cab.

It was canned food. Smith looked at the stamp on top.

"I think it's some kind of stew."

"Take two apiece," ordered Swanson. "We'll eat it when we can."

"Only two?" said Milligan with disappointment.

"Only two," said Swanson sternly. The extra pounds didn't seem like much now, but when they were on foot again—and that could be sooner than they imagined—the added weight would feel like an extra ton.

The other crates yielded a hodgepodge of things. Bandages, flour, more medicines, and with that weird, twisted logic that every military organization seemed to have built into it, a large consignment of harmonicas.

"How do you figure this?" asked Milligan, holding up one of the instruments.

"Simple," said Swanson. "Ever met a supply sergeant who didn't screw up fewer than six times a day?"

"Milligan," said Marquez, "you put that thing near your mouth and you'll get greased."

"How 'bout if I play 'La Cucaracha'?"

"*Particularly* if you play 'La Cucaracha.'"

The last crate yielded a few dozen metal ammunition boxes. Nasty unclipped one cover and found hand grenades. There were, all told, a thousand of them.

"I know," said Nasty, smiling at Swanson, "two apiece."

"Maybe a couple more than that. They'll make a nice big bang when we have to get our hats and leave this party."

Despite the mesmerizing, narcotic jostling of the truck, none of them slept. First off, Swanson wouldn't have allowed it, and even if he had they were too keyed up. They knew that there was a firefight coming and no one wanted to be caught groggy when it started.

Swanson guessed that their speed was somewhere around thirty-five, forty miles an hour. They had traveled for something on three hours when the whole convoy started to slow down. It was 10:30—late mealtime—and Swanson guessed a chance for the convoy commander to switch rear guards.

Swanson's mouth went dry.

"I think this is it," he whispered. "Frank, you're with me. When we stop you go around the passenger side. I'll take the driver. Nasty, try and go over the top through the hatch. Got it?"

"You bet."

"What about us?" asked Wex.

"We're gonna try and do this quiet. If the driver and his buddy cause any trouble, I want you three to go through the roof. Get up through the canvas and get some covering fire going, front side. A few of those wouldn't hurt either." He pointed at the grenades.

"Check."

"They're not going to expect fire to come from one of their own vehicles so I think we have a minute or two to do some real damage. We gotta use that time. Any questions?"

There were none.

"Good luck," said Swanson.

The truck had slowed to a walking pace. Milligan and Swanson dropped lightly off the tailgate and separated, each casually strolling along his assigned side of the truck.

The number-six truck stopped, and then the seventh slowed and rolled to a halt, the puggy nose of the vehicle only ten or twelve yards from the rear of the one in front.

The relief driver was dozing, his head resting against the glass. As the truck stopped, he jerked upright from his slump, yawned, and looked out the window—directly into Milligan's coldly determined eyes. In that split second the man's eyes flicked from the big Irishman's face down to the menacing coach gun and then back to his face. There had been talk of a ruthless band of highly trained American fifth columnists parachuted into the vicinity. The look on the man's face left no doubt as to what he was thinking: this was one of the murdering American bandits. Before Milligan could tug at the door handle, the Russian gave a little shriek and slammed down the lock.

"Goddamn!" hissed Milligan. He raised the stock of the shotgun and pounded the glass with the butt. A spiderweb crack appeared in the pane.

Swanson had no trouble getting the door open on his side of the truck. He snatched the cab door open, reached in, and pulled the driver from his seat. The man fell heavily to the ground. He caught a glimpse of the knife and fought for his life. The sudden confrontation with death brought out untapped wellsprings of strength in the man. Swanson flattened him in the dirt, smelling the bitter scent of fear and panic coming from the writhing soldier. Hands curved like claws raked at Swanson. The Russian's hand closed over the knife blade, slicing the fleshy palm to the bone. A gout of blood splattered over both of them. Swanson rocked the knife back and forth in the man's hand, trying to free it for a final, clean, fatal blow. But that hand, bones glowing like ivory in its bloody nest of flesh and tendon, was working on its own, independent of the pain that coursed through the rest of the Russian's body. It refused to break its maniacal grasp on the blade.

Blindly, Swanson used his free hand to feel around on the road next to him. It closed over a handful of rock a little larger than a baseball. He brought it down sharply on the man's face. Then he pulled back and hit him again.

Kill him. The order burned through Swanson's brain. He raised his gore-slick hand and smashed the man again, for the third time. Blood as purple as a sunset welled up from the smashed bones and squashed eye where the left side of the man's face used to be. One of the blows pushed a sharp shard of bone back into the soft mass of the man's brain. The body under him went limp and Swanson slumped against the truck.

The sudden violent death of the driver went unnoticed by anyone in the forward trucks. Then Swanson heard, as if far off, the screaming of the relief driver. Milligan was still single-mindedly smashing the window, but the Russian had seen the fate that had befallen the driver. Then his brain kicked in and told him that there was another way out.

The hatch.

The window splintered and Milligan pushed his hand through in a shower of diamondlike shards to grope for the lock.

The Russian was halfway through the hatch and screaming, "Americans! Americans!"

Those were his last words. In a perfect parade-ground maneuver—a twist cut—Nasty skewered the relief driver with the bayonet mounted on the nose of the stubby Bushmaster. The man's scream died on his lips. He toppled back through the hatch, a bleeding heap on the seat he had just vacated.

People were running and shouting now. Smith, Wex, Marquez opened up. The little chatter guns dropped two curious but incautious soldiers who came running around from the sides of the number-six truck. They died with a wild look of surprise in their eyes.

Wex lofted a grenade over the truck directly ahead of them, dropping the deadly little projectile in the payload of truck number five. It detonated with a thunderous roar—far louder than a grenade warranted—and a huge fireball shot into the sky. It was the fuel-supply van for the convoy and it blasted a hot wash of intense fire out on all sides. The number-four and -six trucks ignited, frying a couple of soldiers who had been unwise enough to seek refuge under them.

The Bushmasters chattered. An officer or NCO was screaming orders, trying to get his confused men into some sort of fighting order. They were spilling out onto the sides of the road, stumbling and running away from the heat of the fireball. A figure burning brightly ran screaming into the darkness and collapsed in the distance, looking like a far-off campfire.

The men of the *Eagle* concentrated their fire. One spray of their bullets cut down four Russians. The panicked soldiers flopped to their bellies, covering their heads. Most had left their weapons in the now burning trucks. All they could do was take cover and hope that they didn't attract the attention of the unerring marksmen.

As Wex tossed a grenade into their midst, Swanson wrestled the truck into gear and stalled out. The chatter of gunfire was increasing. He swore loudly through clenched teeth as he groped for the ignition. He hit it, gave the truck some gas, and with a lurch they started moving. Milligan pushed himself through the hatch of the truck, adding his own marksmanship to the symphony of hot steel that was emanating from their truck. The Bushmaster in his hands swept up a couple of soldiers cowering in a ditch.

Swanson gunned the engine and pulled past the number-six truck and swerved far off the road to avoid the burning fuel tank and the other burning vehicle. The heat baked them as they passed—Swanson was sure their own canopy was about to explode into flame. A second or two later the flames would reach the open crate of grenades.

It was one way of getting home—to get blasted there in a couple of thousand pieces.

At exactly the wrong moment, Swanson felt the offside truck wheels teeter on the edge of a ditch that ran along the road, then with a shudder the vehicle listed crazily to the left. For one terrible moment he was afraid the whole thing would tip over. He dug the gear into low and the big rear wheels gripped the verge and pushed the truck past the rest of the convoy.

From the roof, Marquez, Wex, Smith, and Nasty were

scattering armfuls of grenades like sowers planting a field. The night was rocked by dozens of explosions. Shrapnel whizzed around the cowering Russians like hailstones, ripping the earth and the bodies that lay on it.

They rumbled by the lead vehicle and the road opened up ahead of them. Milligan was sitting on the cab roof now, looking back at the battle site. In the glow of the burning trucks, he saw an officer shouting into the handpiece of a field radio that was strapped to the back of the operator.

"Nasty! Wex! Get outa the way!"

Milligan flopped belly down on the cab, resting his small gun on the roof bars, and looked carefully down the stubby barrel. In the uncertain light, with the truck bouncing down the road, the supremely confident Milligan didn't rate his chances very high. He squeezed off two rounds. The first smashed the radio and spun the operator full into the path of the second slug, which smashed into his breastbone, picked him up, and threw him down a couple of feet away.

The officer stood blinking, looking at the handpiece of the radio he still held. Milligan dropped him where he stood. Even he had to admit it was a lucky shot.

In Denisov's headquarters a bell rang on one of the old, absurdly slow sixty-six-words-a-minute printers. The bell signaled that an important message was coming down the line.

The printer poured out a few lines of gibberish, then a routing code, then the message began. The KGB had located some additional information on the *Eagle*: Milligan's birthdate, place of birth, and a brief précis of his military history. Then came Wexler's bio.

Denisov stood over the machine reading as the words were spat out onto the roll of yellow paper. Nothing struck him as being of interest until it came to Smith.

"Parents born Leningrad. Y. I. Koslovski (father). H. Berg (mother). Emigrated 1949 Israel. USA 1955. Message ends."

Denisov tore the message off the roll and looked to the long-suffering major who stood at his side.

"I need some more information," said Denisov with a smile.

ELEVEN

The truck rumbled through the night. They were fleeing blindly into the darkness, following the road, going anywhere it chose to meander. Swanson drove like a man in a hurry to get somewhere, although his heavy foot on the gas pedal and his enthusiastic crunching of the stiff gears was born more of the exhilaration of the open road and the lingering battle high than anything else. They had engaged the enemy and taken them down but good. Now they were tearing along an open road, racking up more miles in an hour than they could have in two days' foot travel.

The hoplessness of their situation had burned off in the euphoria of the battle. From the rear of the truck came whoops and shouts as his men relived their triumph. The smell of victory was in the air—at that moment they felt as if they could take on an armored division and win. The six had proven themselves to be a perfect fighting team. It was a good thing, this burst of almost drunken happiness. Let them get high on it, thought Swanson. There were dark days ahead, but a little lightheadedness, a little blowing off steam now would make them a little easier to bear.

"Not too fuckin' shabby," cackled Nasty from the passenger seat, which was still sticky with the relief driver's blood.

"No," agreed Swanson, "we did good." His smile was so big it seemed to light the road ahead of him. The whole country would be crazy to find them now, mad as hornets. And now they had a fix on where they were, more or less.

Let them come, thought Swanson.

They came. The truck blundered over a hill and Swanson found himself face to face with a roadblock. A truck, a sister to the one he drove, had been pulled lengthwise across the road. Soldiers were clustered around it like ticks. A couple of bullets slapped into the nose of the truck like summer rain.

"Nasty!" Swanson didn't have to shout any orders. Nastrazzurro popped through the hatch in the cab, his Bushmaster blazing. Soldiers scattered.

Swanson gunned the engine and yanked the wheel to the left. The truck careened off the road, thrashed through some underbrush, throwing up dirt behind its powerful rear wheels. The sudden shift from open road to open country bounced Nasty down from his perch. Shouts echoed through the night, counterpointed by steady fire from the rear of the truck.

Swanson glanced into his mirror and saw soldiers running and firing. He also saw them dying. Two toppled, then another, then two more. The rest of the pursuers dropped facedown in the dirt and fired from that much safer position. A sudden ragged shuddering rocked the truck. One, maybe two tires had been hit.

Then he saw the town—a few hundred dim lights and some shadows darker than the night.

Swanson didn't hesitate. He stood on the gas and muscled the truck the last three-quarters of a mile across the open country into the town.

It was the sort of town you found in wide open spaces, in prairies and deserts. A couple of main streets, a few wooden houses clustered on the cross streets that led out into the wastes. Once out of the town there was nowhere to go except away from the town. It petered out into nothing a few hundred yards from the last cheap prefab dwelling.

The first bullets from the soldiers at the roadblock had hit the hood and slammed into something essential in the engine. Smoke was pouring out from under the hood, the engine running hot and jagged. The sick bellow of the dying engine seemed to fill the quiet back street. Swanson stamped on the brake and the truck ground to a halt with a death rattle.

"Everybody out!" yelled Swanson.

The five men tumbled out of the truck at their leader's command. They stood in the crossroads for a second, looking around them. The town, flat and regularly laid out, offered nothing in the way of cover. But it didn't really matter which way they went; the little deathly quiet town was beginning to look like a prison as hard to get out of as Alcatraz.

"C'mon," said Swanson, leading the way down the dimmest street. Their flight boots rang on the cracked tar of the street. Headlights—military vehicles—were beginning to flash on the streets, the thundering of engines and the hoarse bark of orders were beginning to crowd the silence.

"We gotta get off the street," said Marquez.

Houses stood close together on both sides of the street.

Swanson's eyes flicked over them. They looked the same; there was nothing to recommend one over the other.

"That one," he said, choosing a tumbledown structure at random.

Swanson walked up to the front door and rattled the handle. Locked.

A voice shouted something hostile from within.

Swanson pounded on the door. The voice called something from inside.

"Smitty, tell him we're the police."

"I can't," said Smitty, agonized. "I don't know the—"

The door swung open to reveal an elderly man in even older pajamas. Swanson rested the barrel of his Bushmaster against the man's hairy chest and pushed him back inside the small house.

The old man's eyes grew wide and his mouth opened and closed a few times, trying to say something, but no sound came out. He looked like an elderly fish dressed for bed. The six crowded into the minute hallway. Very quietly, as if someone were ill in the house, Milligan closed the front door.

A woman in nightclothes, her hair bound up in a kerchief, appeared and saw six filthy, hunted-looking men with guns on her husband and drew her hand to her mouth as if she was trying to stifle a scream.

"Nasty," said Swanson, "cover."

Nasty swung the automatic around until it was only an inch or so from the faded floral-patterned cloth of the woman's nightdress.

"Who else is in the house?" demanded Smith, thinking as he spoke how much he must sound like the KGB or the Gestapo.

The man mumbled something, tears welling into his eyes as he spoke.

"What he say?"

"Daughter," translated Smith, "son-in-law, grand-child."

"Find them."

Wexler and Milligan stomped through the other two small rooms of the house. They found a couple groggily sitting up in bed. They stared, terrified, at the two Americans. The woman jumped from the bed and Milligan tensed, afraid he was going to have to fight her. But she was only going to a crib that stood in one corner of the cramped room. She held the baby protectively; it couldn't have been more than six months old.

They pushed their captives into the small living room and the family sat in a row on the saggy couch and stared unbelieving at these sudden arrivals.

Swanson looked from face to face. There was, understandably, fear there. But it was a hard, palpable fear, terror so plain that it seemed like you could grab a piece and squeeze the panic out of it.

To Swanson it seemed that the baby looked with terror at the six men with guns who had suddenly become part of their lives. Swanson wanted to say something reassuring, but he stopped himself. What could he say? He was the enemy with the power of life or death over them. They would always hate him, they would always fear him. When the soldiers found these six Americans and captured or killed them, these five Russians would be relieved, glad; they would think that they had been rescued, saved from death at the hands of the invaders.

He wanted to tell them that they wouldn't be hurt. But he couldn't make that promise.

"Okay," said Swanson. "Wex, Joe, you stay here and keep them quiet. Nasty, Smitty, Frank, we're gonna take a quiet look around. We have got to figure a way out of this place. If they find us and we start running, we have to be running in the right direction. We meet back here in fifteen minutes. And I mean fifteen. Wex, Joe, if we're not back, this mission is over. Take off as best you can. I don't want anyone hanging around. Okay?"

"Yessir."

"Let's move it."

Wexler and Marquez dragged chairs from the dining room table and set them down in front of the captives.

"Oh God," whispered Wex.

"What's the matter?"

"I don't want to have to shoot these people."

The captives looked at them. They were gray faced with terror. They hoped, like Wex, that they would live to see the end of this night.

Outside, the four men split up. Nasty and Milligan headed for the northern end of town, Smith and Swanson took the southern. Swanson watched his two men dart down the street using the shadows and doorways as cover. In a matter of seconds he couldn't see them. It was as if the night had swallowed them up.

"C'mon," said Swanson, tapping Smith on the shoulder.

They dashed down one of the narrow streets and flattened themselves against a building. A jeep full of soldiers ground slowly by. There was the clatter of static from the radio. Smith poked his head around the corner. The jeep lumbered to a halt at an intersection and stopped there. Soldiers jumped out, weapons at the ready. But instead of fanning out they stayed where they were. The town was being sealed at every corner.

"Dammit," said Swanson. "We haven't got fifteen minutes."

Swanson glanced at the intersection directly in front of them. In a matter of minutes a jeep would occupy that spot.

Swanson could see it all unfolding in his mind. The Russians were calming down. They were beginning to go about this methodically. With the streets sealed, a house-to-house search was next.

"Time," he demanded. "How long have we been gone?"

"Eight minutes."

"*Damn*. The roads are closed. We have to get out in open country. We have to find a back door. Let's move it."

They darted back the way they came, crossed a street, and stepped directly into the glare of headlights.

There was a shout, followed immediately by the chugging blast of a high-caliber machine gun. The big bullets sang in the night and tore gouts of wood out of a sagging wooden building that stood at the corner.

The two Bushmasters returned fire, raking the jeep with fire. The lights went out but the shots continued to zip out of the dark, aiming at the muzzle flashes. Smith reared back and tossed a grenade. The jeep exploded, a bucket of flame, smoke, and screams, lighting the street brighter than the searchlight, brighter than the day. Flames licked onto the roof of the frame houses fronting the street. People yelled and rushed into the street.

But Swanson and Smith weren't around to see it. Panting, they dashed back to their safe house and slammed the door. They collapsed against the wall, their hearts pounding in their chests.

Marquez appeared.

"What happened?"

"Nasty and Milligan. They back?"

"No. We heard shots. . . ."

"That was us," said Smith between gasps for air to calm his heart.

"Shit," said Swanson. He hit the wall with his fist, then looked at his watch. Fourteen minutes. "The Russians?"

"Nice and quiet. Not a peep."

All three men swung around to face the door, automatic weapons at the ready. The door smashed open. A furious firefight almost erupted in the tiny hallway.

"Hold it," gasped Nasty. "Us."

Milligan was right behind him. "They're coming down the street. Searching the houses."

"Did they see you come in here?"

"They'd be here by now if they did."

"Joe, take the door. Smitty, Nasty, Frank, come with me."

They crowded back into the living room. Swanson crossed to the window, parted the thin curtains, and looked out. The family stared at him.

"What's out there?"

The old man spoke.

"He says the garden."

"Then what?"

The old man shrugged. "A road."

"Then?"

"He says nothing."

"What does he mean, nothing?"

"The country."

"Goddamn," said Swanson. "It was right in front of our faces. This is the way out."

Marquez crept into the room. "They're here," he stage whispered. "Sounds like two or three."

As if on cue there was a pounding at the door.

"Okay." Swanson turned to Smith. "You tell him, the old man, that he answers the door. He hasn't heard anything. He hasn't seen anything. He knows nothing. He's been asleep. He so much as whispers and we take down his family. Got it?''

Smith stumbled through his Russian and the old man nodded. The pounding at the door became louder, more insistent.

"Smitty, stand by the door and listen to what he says."

The old man shuffled from the room without looking back at his family.

"C'mon," hissed Nasty, "what's gone wrong?"

"What the hell are you talking about?"

"I open-looped a truck. It should have blown by now. When it goes, everyone is going to head that way."

Smith was listening to the conversation at the door. "Our man is doing fine. Fuck, *I* believe him."

The two soldiers noticed that the old man was trembling with fear. But they were used to that. Everyone who had answered their doors had been terrified. When soldiers with AK-47s knocked on a door in the middle of the night, they knew better than to expect a warm welcome.

"You have seen nothing suspicious?"

"I . . ."

"Come on, old man."

"No, I told you, I was sleeping."

"Who lives here?"

"Me, my wife. My daughter. Her husband. The baby."

"Where are they?"

"Sleeping."

The soldiers seemed satisfied with that. They started to turn away from the door. A helicopter clattered overhead.

"Go back to bed, old man."

Smith heaved a sigh of relief and slumped against the wall.

Just then, before the soldiers had quite turned away, Nasty's booby-trapped truck exploded in the next street over. The ground shook and the night turned yellow. The nerves of the old man, already stretched to the breaking point, snapped.

"In there! In there!" he shrieked. "The bastards have killed my family. The Americans! The Americans!"

"Son of a bitch!" yelled Smith.

The soldiers elbowed the old man out of the way and kicked open the door to the living room. The two men walked straight into the deadly twin barrels of Milligan's shotgun.

Mother and daughter screamed. The family dived for the floor, the baby yelped.

One soldier took more of Milligan's shot than the other. In an instant his features changed from normal to a bloody mass. Shreds of skin, lips, and eyelids dangled and flapped from the caved-in bone structure of his face. He tottered sideways and fell onto the white tablecloth that covered the dining table.

The other toppled back, waving his AK-47 as if not quite able to make out exactly where his target stood. He looked very sad. A burst from Wex's automatic whipped him back to the wall and a second rip pinned him to it. He left a bloody track on the pale yellow wall as he slid down it. By the time he reached the floor, the six had climbed out the window and were pounding through the newly turned earth of the Russians' garden.

The town was alive now, wide awake. A part of it was burning. Jeeps and trucks roared through the streets and the neat intersection barricade had been abandoned. Soldiers ran and fired and shouted at each other. But they were all headed in more or less the same direction—toward the booby-trapped truck that burned furiously. As the soldiers went one way, the fugitives ran at a ninety-degree angle to the Russians, into the open country. It was the perfect application of the create-a-diversion stratagem.

Almost perfect.

From the air the town looked like an ants' nest stirred up by mischievous children. And it was from the air that the six were in the most danger. Those in the helicopter—regular army and as professional a team in their way as were Swanson and his men—were not taken in by the burning truck. The chopper cut across the town, bisecting it, not even deigning to come down for a little closer look at the small inferno.

"Fools," said the pilot into his mouthpiece. "Do you think the Americans would blow up the truck and then stay there?"

The spotter shrugged. The pilot always had an opinion on something, and it usually had something to do with the failings and stupidity of his fellow men, in particular the failings of the conscript army.

"Give me the light," said the pilot.

The powerful spotlight mounted on the underside of the chopper threw a beam straight down, illuminating a vast area. The spotter grasped the movable follow spot mounted on the bar next to his position and sent the white light stabbing out into the darkness.

Nothing. Rooftops, gardens, a few white, thin, curious faces staring up and wondering what catastrophe had visited their little town, a place heretofore so quiet that not even the Third World War could ruffle its calm or wake it from its sound sleep.

The helicopter swung way out from the town, banked steeply on the outskirts, and came back for another look in the narrow streets.

"Wait," said the spotter. "I saw something."

The six watched the chopper pass overhead as the edge of the carpet of light washed over them. They dived for the safety of darkness, then watched the blinking tail wink away back toward the town.

As soon as the chopper started a second and steeper bank over the town and headed back for open country—for them—they knew they were in trouble.

"He saw us," said someone.

The six started running again. The pilot of the helicopter kicked his craft over to starboard, lost seventy-five feet of altitude and came roaring back at them.

"He's seen us," said Nasty.

Instinctively, they all realized at once that it would be pointless to try and outrun the beast. The country before them was featureless except for a clump of trees that seemed ten thousand miles away. If they tried to run for it, the chopper would cut them down. They had to stay and fight.

The movable light controlled by the spotter jabbed out toward them. Suddenly the area around the six went from darkest night to brightest day. It was the unnatural light of a night game in a stadium back home. Not only did the light illuminate the field, but it challenged the night itself, throwing the dark way back in the distance.

"Down!" yelled Swanson.

The helicopter charged at them, a screaming, fire-spitting insect, like something out of an old, cheap Japanese horror movie. The twin machine guns mounted under it opened up, chopping up the gorse and bracken. The Bushmasters returned fire, but they didn't have the power to smash the delicate machine that whined above them. The best they could hope for was a lucky shot, a slug in the fuel tank or the pilot. Milligan managed to stitch a neat line of holes across the bulbous nose, splintering the air-speed spine that thrust out from the prow like the whisker on an old dog.

The pilot did not panic. He eased down on the cyclic and the helicopter drifted up to three hundred meters. The white light poured down on them like a waterfall. The Bushmasters—all except for Milligan's—kept up their fire.

"Cut it," screamed Frank. "It's outa range. You're wasting ammunition."

"Then let's go," yelled Swanson. All they could do now was make a dash for the trees and hope that some of them made it. Five of the six jumped to their feet. A burst of machine-gun fire threw them down again.

Very clearly, Swanson thought, We haven't got a prayer.

Very calmly, Milligan rose to one knee as if he were going to propose old-fashioned style. He raised a weapon, but not his Bushmaster. The grip of the stolen weapon was still sticky with the blood of the Russian soldier he had taken it from. He summoned up all he knew about the AK-47. Gas operated, 7.62 caliber, thirty-shot clip. Range: four hundred meters, semi-auto.

"Let's see if you're all you're cracked up to be," he whispered as if talking to a woman who had a hell of a reputation for being good in bed.

It was. Milligan emptied all thirty rounds into the chopper. The first six killed the light and passed through that into the underbelly of the machine. The sudden pounding surprised the chopper pilot and inadvertently he lost twenty or thirty meters of altitude. That put the chopper right in Milligan's wheelhouse.

The second six bullets opened up the observer's chest. Bone chips crackled against the cabin walls like sleet. Milligan pumped the last eighteen slugs into the canopy in the vicinity of the pilot. The canopy shattered in a snowstorm of plexiglass. The chopper rocked left, then right, then sank to the ground, the rotors chopped up the ground, and that drove the machine's shattered body over on its side. The night was filled with smoke and sparks and flames and the screams of dying machinery and men.

"Hell of a weapon," Milligan could be heard saying as the six melted into the darkness.

TWELVE

Skill, training, instinct—all of the best qualities of the six, the things that made them different, that had carried them so successfully so far—all crumbled under a single demand their bodies now made on them. Sleep.

They had marched, fought, run, fought, hidden, fought, and run again all in the space of twenty-four hours. Their battle-toughened bodies were strong, but they could only take so much. The last seven or eight miles covered that night finished them.

As the dawn came licking around the edges of the new gray day, they collapsed. Not even the inhospitable terrain could prevent them from hitting the ground and sleeping. They had blundered into a marsh that seemed to stretch to the horizon. They splashed through stagnant pools and tall reeds, across squashy grassland that reminded Swanson of coastal tidal flats. In a huge patch of reeds that rose taller than any of them, Swanson called a halt.

"This seems as good a place as any," he said hoarsely.

Groggily, the men sank to their knees. The ground was wet and uncomfortable.

"Duty?" asked Marquez.

"Not today," said Swanson. "No one could keep their eyes open. If he could, he'd never be able to raise the others." He didn't reveal his other reason for not posting a guard. If the Russians found them now, there was nothing he and his men could do. They were low on ammo, so they couldn't expect to fight them off. And they were too tired to run.

"We're in a jam," he said, staring at them through red-rimmed eyes. "How many rounds do we have between us?" They patted their pockets and looked into their packs.

"Maybe twenty total," said Milligan. "And I got some shells for the shotgun."

"Couple of grenades left," said Nasty.

"Just checking," said Swanson, his worst fears confirmed. He wished they had known enough not to go hammering away at that chopper. He wondered how many rounds had been wasted that way. "We'll rest today and try moving tonight."

He settled himself on the wet ground and wondered if he would wake up looking into the mouth of an AK-47. Right at that moment he didn't care.

He didn't awaken to a sight but a sound. It was the heavy slap of helicopter rotors against the air, followed by the whine of the powerful engine that pushed the thing through the sky.

The sound roused them all. Swanson looked from man to man. They looked awful. Their eyes were bloodshot and their faces were gaunt and yellow under the heavy growths of beard and the pancake dirt. Their hair was matted down on their heads with dirt and dried sweat. Hands with jet-black nails fingered weapons.

Beyond the scream of the chopper was an even more chilling sound. Voices. Shouts. Soldiers were invading the swamp. There were only two pieces of good news, as far as Swanson could make out: he couldn't hear any ground transport, meaning the soldiers were on foot, and there were no dogs, although Swanson wasn't sure how effective they would have been in the swamp.

But he had some good news. If the men of the *Eagle* were going to be found, the soldiers would have to stomp through every inch of that swamp. That gave them some time, if nothing else.

Swanson gestured to his men to stay down. Slowly he raised his tired bones off the ground and tried to peer above the reeds. He could see nothing. The unseen chopper clattered away into the distance.

Bent almost double, Swanson darted through the reeds a way, losing a little cover in his quest for a glimpse of the men who were stalking them. At the edge of the cluster of reeds, where they thinned out and came down to about chest height, he risked a four or five second look at the unwelcoming and dangerous world around him. He didn't like what he saw. The swamp seemed to be alive with soldiers and they all seemed to be headed toward him. He was relieved to see that they had not formed an unbroken cordon. There weren't enough troops for that. Instead, there were patrol groups—threes and fours—moving through the swamp, gingerly poking here and there, plainly afraid of suddenly coming face to face with a band of murderous Americans.

Obviously, men who could destroy a convoy, half wreck a town, and shoot down a helicopter and escape into the bargain were men to be reckoned with. Someone had heard there were as many as a hundred of them.

Swanson saw that the swamp was enormous, many square miles, though how many he couldn't guess. And though the numbers of soldiers looking for them was substantial, they were plainly inadequate to the task of searching every inch. As Swanson faded back into the reeds, he guessed they still had a chance—like all the other chances on this mission it was a slim one, but the fact that one existed at all gave him heart, if not hope.

The helicopter whined overhead. He wondered if it had an infrared detector. If it did he assumed that the large body of troops would throw it off.

His five men looked up expectantly when he returned to their small, swampy campsite.

"Nothing much," he whispered, "but I don't think we're gonna be doing much traveling today."

The men nodded, but they were disappointed. A day not spent moving was one more day they had to spend in Russia. But given their fatigue, maybe a day's inactivity wasn't such a bad thing.

"One piece of good news," said Marquez.

Swanson raised his eyebrows inquiringly.

"We forgot these." He tapped the sidearm strapped to his thigh.

Swanson nodded. As far as he could recall, not one of them had fired his pistol since this whole crazy thing had begun. It wasn't much, but it was something.

All day they crouched there. They didn't eat or talk. They scarcely breathed. No one moved suddenly, not even to slap at the mosquitoes that began in small numbers, but as word spread among their ranks of the still targets to be found in the center of the swamp, their numbers increased until they were coming in battalions. Swanson watched as the features of his men changed under the onslaught of tension, stress, and mosquitoes. The first two factors acted as a vise tightening their muscles, hollowing their cheeks, pinching their mouths into constant worried frowns. The bites of the bloodthirsty insects had the opposite effect. Every bite seemed to swell. Big ugly red hummocks made their hands and forearms fat and gave their faces the aspect of prizefighters after a career of taking hard punches to the head.

As the day wore on—this had to be the longest one yet—Swanson could tell they were fighting to control themselves. The simple relief that jumping up, moving, screaming, swearing would bring would be immense. To suffer in silence was the greatest torture. But they bore it. Barely.

Finally, as the sun began to sink low in the sky, they could stand it no longer. Swanson decided that they were going to have to do something, anything, to cut short the torture. As he made that decision, Milligan tensed. He held out a hand, cautioning the rest of them to hold still and be quiet—as if they hadn't been doing just that all day. Milligan crawled out of the patch to look around and returned in a minute or two.

He held up four fingers and pointed. Four soldiers coming their way.

Swanson slid his knife out of the sheath and held it up.

His men nodded. Five more knives came out of the belts like snakes out of their lairs. Swanson pointed at Milligan, Nasty, Marquez, and then himself. He gestured to Smith and Wexler; they would be lookouts.

They heard the soldiers talking among themselves as they approached the thicket. They were complaining about the mosquitoes, the foul water that filled their boots, the fact that they had only had a half hour rest all day and that they had a hard-assed NCO lording it over them as if he were a general. They were not paying much attention. They had all agreed that the Americans were long gone.

One shit his pants when Nasty's dirty hand closed firmly over his mouth.

Swanson's men reared like striking cobras. They attacked from behind just as they had been taught years before in their close-combat training. None of them had thought about it, much less practiced it, since basic, but the need to kill had made them experts. Four hands closed over four mouths. Four blades sank deep, sliding into the kidney zone of the four victims. The men sagged in their arms.

For a second Marquez staggered under the weight of his victim, then he imitated Swanson, who did it right, and followed his corpse to the ground, going down with it instead of being pulled off balance.

One of the soldiers gurgled. Swanson cut his throat. He was a young man. His brown eyes looked sadly at the blade as it passed his face on its way to his neck. As the blade sank in, it seemed suddenly that they were hiding in a swamp not of stagnant water but of rich, newly tapped blood. The last few spastic pumps of the young man's heart shot gout after gout of scarlet blood onto the reeds, onto the damp ground, over Swanson's hands. He turned away from his victim as bloody as a butcher after a hard day's work. The killing had not affected him at all. He was getting used to it.

He looked inquiringly at Smith and Wexler. They shook their heads. As best as they could tell, no one had seen the four soldiers fall. One moment they were there. A second later they were gone.

Nasty pulled the pins from two grenades and carefully laid two of the bodies on them, the weight of the dead men holding the spring clips on the bombs in place. Swanson looked at him.

Nasty shrugged as if to say, "Can't hurt."

Swanson pulled his men together as if they were a football team going into a huddle.

It was hard to speak after being silent for so long.

"We gotta get out here," he croaked.

"Amen," said Milligan.

"We're gonna have to move a space away from these bodies. Not far. Hundred yards, two hundred if we can. When night comes, they'll probably"—he broke off as the chopper passed overhead—"probably call in their troops. They are going to notice that these guys have gone missing. My guess is that they'll get pretty bullshit. Frank, what weapons were they carrying?"

"Four shiny AK-47s. Two clips each."

"Okay, I'll take a Bushmaster. You too, Joe."

They exchanged weapons and then, with Swanson leading the way, they crawled on their bellies on the slimy ground to another thicket of reeds, one that Swanson hoped had been searched already. There they sat and waited for the sun to set, for the sky to darken. Swanson had no trouble deciding this *was* the longest day of his life. It seemed like it would never end.

THIRTEEN

An hour or so after the sun had set, it sounded as if the Russians had bowed to the failing light and decided to call the search off for the night.

Orders were issued on all sides by sergeants. They ran around barking like sheep dogs circling their flocks, keeping their dim charges together. It quickly became obvious that the soldiers in the field were to spend the night where they were and to recommence the search on that line the next morning. Swanson guessed that by the next day more troops would have been flown in, more choppers brought up. The trap would begin to snap shut, the noose would cinch a little tighter. They couldn't relax—if they were going to get out of this then a bold move was needed. Swanson had a feeling that he knew exactly what needed to be done. Bold was a good name for it, but suicidal was better.

He caught the eyes of his men and moved them closer in to the huddle.

"Change of plan," he whispered. "When they find the bodies we run, but we run toward them."

The five looked at their chief, wondering if he hadn't been in the swamp a little too long.

He tried to explain it as fast as he could.

"They're going to be on our tail tomorrow but good. And they'll be better and stronger the day after that. We have to lose them outright. We double back through the line and then look to see if there isn't a way around it. See?"

They saw. Five heads nodded. But running straight into them—that was a little too much like the Charge of the Light Brigade.

"They won't know we're coming," said Swanson, trying to reassure them. "Any questions?"

No questions.

"Good. Just wait for the shit to start flying."

They nodded. That was usually the signal to start work.

It was a strange experience for a group of professional soldiers to sit concealed and listen to other soldiers going about the task of making camp just a few hundred yards away. Swanson didn't understand the words, but he guessed the meaning without difficulty: NCO abusing, surly soldiers not knowing why they were there and resenting the abuse.

"But why, Sarge, I don't get it. . . ."

"Don't ask why, shithead, just do it."

Or the Russian equivalent.

Swanson could imagine the soldiers eating bad, cold food, sleeping in a damp rack, wondering why the hell they had to sleep in a lousy swamp. How come a swamp? Why not a nice dry field someplace? A swamp! A fucking swamp! And this is food? Call this fuckin' shit food? A dog couldn't eat this crap! Eating shitty food in a fuckin' swamp. Man, the army sucks. . . .

And around and around and around. They would talk about it until the service visited a fresh outrage on them and gave them something new to complain about.

When the NCOs had chased around and yelled enough to direct even the thickest recruit to his place, it was immediately apparent that something had gone wrong. A half dozen sets of stern, all-seeing sergeant eyes saw that something—worse, *someone*—was missing. As soon as this fact sank in, the shouting and ordering about began on an even louder, more frenzied level. The soldiers were being organized into squads. They were being made to slosh around in the swamp as if it were a parade ground.

Swanson could imagine the officers standing to one side, looking worried but aloof, letting the noncoms figure out what was going on, praying that nothing would be found wrong with their platoon. Hanging around somewhere was a senior commanding officer with an aide along as his pilot fish. The commander was probably getting angrier with the passage of each minute. His aide was probably shooting nervous glances at his chief and hoping that he wouldn't take the whole fiasco out on him.

The soldiers counted off. The different voices, the cracked and squeaky voices of conscripts, the growl of grizzled veterans, echoed into the night. It was like calling the roll in a school yard.

"One."

"Two."

"Three."

"Four."

And then back to one again. By the time they had all counted off, it was obvious that there were four men missing. There was silence as NCOs reported to officers and the field officer took the bad news to the commander. Then the whole thing was repeated in reverse. The chief gave orders to the exec, who took them to the platoon commanders, who told the NCOs to get busy. The sergeants gave their orders in very loud voices.

That was it. The six men tensed. The search was on again. Tongues of bright white light licked the tops of the reeds and stabbed into the sky. Sullen soldiers who had already spent all day wandering around in the swamp, brackish water slopping over the tops of their boots, looking for men who weren't there, stumbled forth again.

Not fifteen minutes later the chopper returned. When the search had been called off the last time, the helicopter had zipped away to find a landing spot on dry land. Its crew had to be pulled from a mess hall back in town and sent forth again. They were complaining as much as the soldiers on the ground, but at least they could conduct the search and sit down at the same time.

Under cover of the chopper noise, Swanson spoke.

"Frank, when we move, can you take out the light on the chopper. One shot. No more."

"Yeah," said Milligan.

It took them four long, cold hours to find the bodies. The four corpses were lying facedown in the ooze, all of them set in the middle of a pool of their own gore. Flies and mosquitoes sucked at the blood as if it were an insect version of Thanksgiving. The insects were gorged and lazy with the blood. The six soldiers who located the bodies ran their flashlights over them, not quite able to believe what they were seeing. One of them doubled over and was sick.

A sergeant bustled forward. "Mama's boy," he said.

He turned over two bodies and was sliced to ribbons by the exploding grenades.

"That's it," said Swanson.

Milligan peered through his sights, aiming at the helicopter that was coming in low and slow and lit up like a Christmas tree. He squeezed off one round and the light went out abruptly. Then Milligan committed a court-martial offense; he disobeyed his commanding officer. He fired another round. It was a blade shot and a good one. The heavy bullet clipped a slice out of one of the rotors. The pilot fought with his buck craft but couldn't control the low stall. The machine slammed into the ground, splitting into a dozen pieces on impact.

The crew of the *Eagle* was off and running. So was every other man within half a mile. The great military beast goes a little crazy when things don't go as planned. In a matter of minutes there had been some unexplained explosions, then without warning the chopper light went out. A second or two later the machine just fell out of the sky. *What the hell is going on?* the Russians wondered.

Confusion and panic swept over the Russian field force. They did what heavily armed men, suddenly bereft of discipline and order, do. They started shooting. They shot at one another, they shot at shadows, they shot at places where the wind rustled the reeds. Muzzle flashes zipped in and out of the tall reeds, the smoke from the guns mixing with the acrid, electric smoke pouring from the crashed copter. There were cries of pain and panic.

Through it all sprinted Swanson and his men. They were ready for attack, but none came. To anyone who might have noticed them, they were nothing more than another group of armed men running somewhere—exactly where, no one could say. Except Swanson and his men. They knew where they were and they knew where they were going. They even had a good idea of where they would strike next. They were men with a plan, men with a purpose. The Russians were rabble.

They covered a mile or so with relative ease. The rushing soldiers did nothing to stop them. In fact, no one would recall having seen them. But it wasn't a stroll on the beach either. They blundered in the darkness, sinking knee deep in mud or sloshing through shallow, stagnant pools. Reeds whipped at their faces and tore their clothing, opening up tiny cuts.

They passed through the half-made camp—no Russian soldier would sleep there that night—and beyond, leaving the sounds of confusion and panic behind them. Their lungs were burning, their hearts pounding, but still they ran, striving to get out of the stinking swamp, pounding away in an attempt to get to the security of dry land and good cover.

They were almost there. They had almost reached the line of tall trees that marked the end of the swamp and the beginning of firm ground. They were closing on their objective. They had almost made it.

Marquez was running just behind Swanson. He put his booted foot down on some deceptively firm-looking ground. It gave way beneath him. He sank to his knee, the weight of his body, heavy with the momentum of flight forcing itself down on the fragile suspension of the joint. He felt something snap in his knee and ankle and a pain shot straight up his leg and exploded in his brain. It had looked to the four men behind him as if his leg had bent forward in a way a knee was not designed to bend. Marquez whipped back like a sapling in a high wind and fell to the ground.

"Goddamn," he gasped, both hands reaching down to free his trapped leg.

The other five stopped on the sloppy ground and looked down worriedly at their fallen comrade. Marquez rolled back and forth, looking as if he were trying to squeeze the pain from his tortured leg.

"Mother fucker," he moaned.

"Joe," said Swanson, kneeling at his side, "take your hands away, let me see." He pried Marquez's hands away from his leg and gently felt his way around the knee.

"Holy shit," hissed Marquez, wincing in pain. "Hey, Jamie, just use a fuckin' knife, why don't you?"

"Sorry. Nothing broken, I don't think."

"Jamie," said Nasty, "we gotta move."

Swanson shot a glance back toward the swamp. "Can you make it to the trees?"

"I'll try, man," said Marquez. His face was ashen. With great effort he pulled himself to a sitting position.

Suddenly Milligan elbowed his way up to Marquez. "Here," he said, "hold this." He dumped his Kalashnikov and shotgun into Wexler's arms and knelt down next to Marquez. Frank spat on his hands and took a deep breath. He grabbed Marquez and swung him up onto his broad shoulders as if he were a bag of cement. Then, like a weight lifter working on a straight press, he stood up.

"He ain't heavy," said Milligan, "he's my brother."

FOURTEEN

They stayed in the cover of the forest during all that remained of that night and well into the next day. They slept undisturbed and then they ate and then they slept some more. They made a bandage out of the tattered sleeves of their flight suits, and as carefully as they could they bound up Marquez's swollen knee and ankle.

When they asked him if it hurt, he always said the same thing.

"Naw, not too bad."

"Stupid question," murmured Milligan.

Smith almost blasted Marquez that night while he was standing guard duty. He had heard someone near their camp and, luckily before letting rip with some slugs from the Kalashnikov, he investigated. He found Marquez hobbling away. He claimed that he was just taking a leak, but they all knew what he was planning on doing. He was going away, trying to sacrifice himself so that the others would have a better shot at escape. He knew that from here on he was just a drag on them, a burden. He was no good to anyone anymore.

Swanson had had a quiet word with Marquez.

"Let me tell you something, Joe," he said. "If we wake up some morning and you're not around, we're gonna come looking for you. And that's dangerous. That will slow us down."

Marquez nodded. "Sorry."

At dusk they started out again, leaving the cover of the scrubby forest. They found Marquez a stout stick, and he used that as a cane. Milligan walked next to Marquez, letting him lean on him.

But progress was slow. They all knew that Marquez needed proper medical attention, good food, and rest. They all needed it, but Marquez needed it more. Most of all he needed time, time to let the wound heal. And time they didn't have. All of those things were a thousand miles and a whole world away.

Marquez's injury depressed them all. They were moving too slowly; the extraordinary progress they had been making ceased.

But it was more than mere mileage that made Marquez's injury so dispiriting. Because of it, suddenly, perhaps for the first time, they saw in stark light the danger, the precariousness of their position. A single slight mishap, a messed-up leg, something that would have been hardly noticeable in what they still thought of as real life, seemed now to be a giant catastrophe. A serious bullet wound, a broken leg, the loss of Nasty's sextant would mean one of two things: capture or death. It was that simple.

By midnight they had closed on the town they had escaped from two nights before.

"You gotta figure this is the last place they're gonna look for us."

"Exactly," said Swanson.

They found shelter in the drainage pipe that ran under a railway embankment. It was cramped and uncomfortable, but it was dry—drier than the swamp at least.

"Four of you stay here. Me and Smitty are going to take a look around," said Swanson. "That okay with you, Arnie?"

"I have no problem with that, sir," said Smith.

"If my hunch is right, this town is going to be more or less clean of soldiers. They're probably still out in that swamp. I think they'll guess that we ran away from the town rather than toward it."

Nasty was a little pissed off at being left behind. "What should we do?"

"Praying is good," said Swanson.

They clambered up the embankment and walked the tracks looking like a pair of hoboes—heavily armed hoboes. They crossed the open ground that surrounded the town and found themselves once again in the narrow, dirty streets they had shocked awake and fled from nights before. The streets had the same deathly quiet. There was no human sound; no singing, cursing drunk stumbling home. No engines. No sudden shout from someone whose sleep was filled with nightmares. No dog barked.

There were no cars, no trucks, no vehicles of any kind parked on the streets. Swanson had vaguely thought that they might be able to steal some sort of vehicle and take to the road. In the soulless quiet of the dark street in that tiny, scared town, he realized that hot-wiring a truck and driving out would be about as inconspicuous as singing "The Star-Spangled Banner" in the middle of the town square.

Swanson's heart sank. His plan, such as it was, was

unraveling. They couldn't strike out for the country—
Marquez couldn't travel very far on foot—and they couldn't
get any ground transport.

They crept through the dark streets, keeping close to the
shadows, moving like rats too scared to dart out into the
daunting open spaces of the streets. They wandered,
unwilling to return to their comrades and report the bad
news.

Then they found the station.

It was a relic of a bygone time, a delicate nineteenth
century gingerbread railway station with peaks and gables
and gargoyles. It had the self-important aspect of a totally
insignificant building upon which endless pointless care had
been lavished.

The twentieth century had intruded in the form of a sturdy
cyclone fence that surrounded the siding to the station's left.
The enclosed area was a confusion of sheds and piles of tree
trunks to be finished into lumber somewhere else. The
jumble was overseen by a lone crane. Standing on the single
track was a railway locomotive coupled to three or four
logging flatcars. The tiniest wisp of smoke licked out of the
engine's funnel.

Here at last was a sound. From fifty yards away Swanson
and Smith could hear the regular scrape and thump of a man
working to fill the furnace of the old coal burner with fuel.
Light was seeping into the eastern sky like a stain. Plainly,
the engineer was stoking up his machine for his day's work.

"Any idea how to run a train?" asked Swanson.

"What do you think?"

"I didn't think so. Me neither."

Even if it's never happened to you before, there is
something about the feeling of a gun pressed into your back
that tells you immediately what it is. The stoker on the train

was bent over his pile of coal when Swanson jammed the nose of his Colt into his back.

"Tell him what to do, Smitty."

"C'mon, Grandfather," said Smith, "stand up straight and be silent."

The fireman slowly straightened, holding his hands away from his side. He had the wide-lipped, downturned mouth of the sad clown in a circus. The effect was completed by his bulbous nose, which was red as a beet, telling of the man's fondness for strong drink.

Rather than frightened, he looked melancholy, deeply sad that a hard life should suddenly become that much more difficult with the arrival of two Americans with guns. Men who wanted his train. He looked sadly at them. Then a tear as fat as a grape slid down his mottled cheek.

"Oh shit," said Smith.

"Tell him that we're not going to hurt him, that he must do as we say."

Smith translated and the man nodded. He understood. It was much as he imagined they would say.

"Where does this train go?"

The man mumbled something.

"Someplace I didn't catch the name of," said Smith, "but it's in the forest."

"Close enough. Tell him to get it moving."

"He says it's too early. Usually he leaves at six o'clock."

"Now, why would he tell us that?" said Swanson. "Why would he not want us to attract attention? Or does someone come on duty at six? A stationmaster maybe. Or a foreman. Ask him that."

"I can't because I don't know how."

"Okay, okay, just tell him never mind what time it is. Let's get moving."

Smith nudged the man toward the shiny brass controls. "Go now, Grandfather. Take us for a ride."

The old man sighed, eased off on the brakes, and tugged at the throttle. The iron wheels slipped on the track a couple of times. Steam poured from the stack with a chuff-chuff like something in a children's story. Then the old engine moved forward. It rolled out of the yard like an arthritic old man getting out of bed on a cold morning. The rods and pistons worked jerkily, as if they were uncertain about whether or not they wanted to work that day at all.

The first leg of the track was laid parallel to one of the major streets of the little town. As the engine and its cars rolled alongside the street, an early riser pushing his bicycle down the street shouted something at the driver of the engine. The old man, acutely aware of Smith and Swanson lying on the footplate with guns aimed at his heart, just shrugged and smiled.

"What did the guy say?" Swanson stage whispered.

"He said, 'Right on time.'"

Swanson wagged a finger at the driver as if he were reprimanding a child. The driver gave a can't-blame-me-for-trying shrug.

They were a half mile out of town when Smith told the driver to slow down.

"Why? I never stop here."

"Don't argue. Do as you're told," said Smith in flawless Russian with a pronounced Leningrad accent. He was doing an imitation of his mother. She would always say those words when he disobeyed her.

The Russian was impressed. "Your language is quite good."

"Don't change the subject. Do as you're told," he quoted his mother again.

The driver vented some steam and leaned on the brake.

Smith clambered down the side of the embankment while the engine snuffed and snorted like a cart horse. He narrowly avoided getting blown away by Milligan, who crouched at the entrance of the pipe.

"Get down, mother fucker! There's a train up there."

Smith grinned. "I know. It's ours."

Milligan carried Marquez up the steep slope and Joe was hauled up onto the footplate by Swanson. He laid him down on the coal pile in the tender and made him as comfortable as possible. Marquez hated it. He felt like an old man.

"Get this thing moving," ordered Swanson.

The driver shrugged and eased the throttle open and the little train shuffled down the track, the flatcars rumbling behind.

The clattering of the engine and the monotonous scrape of the driver's shovel as he stoked the furnace wrapped them in a cocoon of metallic noise—nothing from the outside world could penetrate.

If the pilot of the helicopter closing in on them had realized where they were, a single missile could have blown the train off the tracks and saved the U.S.S.R. a lot of bother. He could even have stopped the train by blowing out a piece of the railbed. But he, being a well-trained, cautious helicopter pilot in the Soviet Air Force—an organization where personal initiative is neither rewarded nor encouraged—chose the simplest, stupidest course of action. He radioed the position of the train and then dropped a couple of hundred feet and came in low for a look.

The men were standing on the footplate of the train as the chopper came swooping in like a prehistoric bird. Swanson felt the skin on his neck creep up as he braced for the line of tracers that he was sure would come spitting into the metal box they were now trapped in. But they didn't come.

Milligan came up shooting. The Kalashnikov bucked a

half dozen times and tore a chunk out of the tail of the retreating helicopter. The pilot felt his craft jolted by the slugs and fought for a second or two to control his ship as it swung port to starboard and back to port like a pendulum on a grandfather clock that had been jolted into insane motion. Apart from that momentary loss of control, the bullets passed through the fuselage without doing any damage except to the pilot's pride.

"C'mon back, asshole," said Milligan, screaming at the metallic dragonfly getting smaller in the sky. The pilot banked on the northern side of the train and faded back, shadowing the train from behind.

"Down!" shouted Swanson. He grabbed the trouser leg of the driver, pulling him down on the metal flooring of the train cab.

Bullets from the copter whipped over the coal pile like a vicious wind, making a sound like a bunch of bolts pureed in a blender. The big bullets flattened themselves against the thick plating. Coal chips flew like shrapnel; fine grains of bullet-driven anthracite flew through the air. Some of the pieces caught Nasty in the fleshy part of his thigh, tearing his already tattered trouser leg. The coal chips and the threads got hopelessly mixed up in the meat of his leg. A few slivers caught Swanson along the cheekbone, producing a gout of blood out of all proportion to the seriousness of the wound.

Milligan heard the chopper flash over them again and cursed.

"Goddamn, man, gimme another chance like that! The belly of that fat fuck went over at thirty mother-fuckin' feet!"

But the pilot followed the orders that were crackling into his earphone. Keep the train in view, do not attempt to attack. Await reinforcements.

* * *

Denisov was pleased. Stationed at a local military headquarters near the town where the Americans had shown up, he sensed the mission was coming to an end. As a soldier, he could not help but admire the skill with which the breakout from the swamp had been executed. He was looking forward to meeting this Major Swanson.

Denisov's major smiled. He hated Denisov so much that he half hoped the Americans got away, if only to take the arrogant young colonel down a peg or two.

Denisov rapped out an order. "Transport."

The major saluted and fled.

Milligan was lying flat on the coal tender, looking at the helicopter a half mile behind him. He watched the chattering beast with the same intensity as a cat staring at a canary safely locked away in a cage out of reach. He slithered off the coal and sat next to Swanson, who was pressing a sleeve against his cheek.

"I'd like to buy that chopper, sir."

"I'll give you a good deal on it," said Swanson. "She's all yours. Drive it off the lot."

"She's also outa range."

Swanson looked over his shoulder. "Just trailing us. What's it got in the way of weaponry?"

"Machine guns we know about. Looks like he's got some air-to-air or -surface rockets."

"And we're in range, right?"

"Hell, yes!"

"That tell you something?"

"Tells me he's been called off. Waiting for reinforcements, waiting for them to throw a switch somewhere up ahead."

"Which means they want us alive," put in Smith.

"Which means were gonna have to disappoint them,"

Nasty said between gritted teeth. He was doing his best to attend to his ragged wound.

"Frank, if we can get that chopper close, can you take it down?" Swanson asked.

"If it goes over the way it did last time, I can't miss. The problem is getting in range."

"No problem," said Swanson. "Smitty, time to speak some more Russian."

The plan was simplicity itself. It was nothing more than a fake-out, NBA style. Smith informed the white-faced driver that he was to increase the speed of the engine to its absolute maximum. As coal was shoveled into the furnace by Milligan and Wexler and as more and more steam was built up in the boiler, the driver began to look even more worried. Finally he could stand it no more. He broke into a hurried babbling directed at Smith.

"I don't know what you are saying, old man."

The driver gave up on words and pantomimed a dramatic, cataclysmic explosion.

"What's he saying?" demanded Swanson.

"He says that if we go any faster we're going to blow the boiler."

"Tell him it's not for much longer. Does he know what else he has to do?"

"Yep."

"Good. Wait for the order."

The pilot looked over at his co-pilot and smiled as the train picked up speed.

"Do they really think they can outrun us?"

"They are trying," replied the co-pilot, "but they are only wasting coal."

"What do they care? They stole it."

The co-pilot laughed. The pilot eased forward on the throttle and gained speed considerably.

"Milligan," shouted Swanson, "you all secure?"

Milligan sat with his back to the steel bulkhead, his strong legs thrust out in front of him and braced and locked against the lip of the coal tender. He was wedged in tight. He slapped a clip into the AK-47.

"Ready," he said. He raised his weapon and drew a bead on the bubble dome of the chopper.

"Rest of you, hold tight."

The remaining men grabbed something and held on, bracing themselves as best they could.

"Hit it, Smitty."

Smith yelled an order to the driver, who shrugged and slammed on the brakes. The big iron wheels froze, the tie rods locked, and the whole contraption slid along the rails like a sled on patchy ice. The speed dropped dramatically. The boiler clanked and the driver dived for the stop valve, venting steam in a vast cloud.

The sudden stop took the chopper completely by surprise. It happened too quickly for the pilot to use his own air brakes or for him to swing out of the path of Milligan's gun sights. The pilot had no alternative but to keep on course, overshooting the train, coming in low. Once in range, he never had a prayer.

Milligan didn't hesitate. The Kalashnikov spoke with a deadly authority. He pumped eight shots into the canopy of the copter, the big slugs tearing the control panel into jagged pieces. A chunk of the altimeter whipped through the tight space of the cockpit and tore into the co-pilot's muscled neck. Hot blood filled the flight deck. Blood splashed over the shattered canopy. The man's mouth opened, trying to give voice to a scream of pain and terror, but the lump of metal and glass embedded in his flesh had crushed and snapped his vocal cords. He took his hands off the controls and gripped his throat, his fingers scrabbling in his warm blood as he tried to tear the obstruction free.

Milligan peppered the cockpit with shot. A lucky bullet nailed the rudder linkage at the pilot's feet. The Russian felt his gear go stiff and hard. He threw his weight behind the controls, and just as he passed over the cab of the train he pushed his screaming, wounded machine to starboard.

Milligan squeezed off two more shots. His last one did the trick. A steel-jacketed bullet clipped the rocket on the rack just to the pilot's left. The explosive within detonated and the helicopter, with a flash as bright as lightning, blew into thousands of burning pieces. Wreckage rained down on the wasteland next to the railway tracks in a wide-scattered ring of burning rubble. In the very center of the circle, pieces of flesh, great weighty chunks of body burned like a grease fire in a deep fryer.

The six Americans and the driver stared at the remains of the chopper.

"Good shooting, Frank," said Swanson.

"All part of the job."

"Modesty. It suits you," laughed Nasty.

Smitty got the driver to work. With trembling hands he set the controls, stoked up the engine, and eased the train down the tracks. The driver looked sadder than ever. And why shouldn't he? thought Swanson. An enemy had just scored a very impressive victory. It would be the same at home if an American had seen a Russian make a USAF chopper crash and burn.

The sudden disappearance of the helicopter from the radio airwaves told the two choppers coming up to aid their comrade that he had been shot out of the sky. There was a brief conversation between the pilots of the two Mi-240 battle helicopters as they closed fast on the train.

"When the orders came through," said the lead pilot, "static broke up part. Did you get it?"

The second chopper pilot knew what his colleague was getting at.

"I didn't copy. We were to find the train with the bandits aboard, then the transmission broke up."

"Atmospheric interference is very bad today," said the first pilot conversationally. "I assume we are to attack and destroy."

"Exactly."

The chopper pilots knew that these Americans had a remarkable talent for destroying helicopters. They had accounted for three. This, they decided, must stop. Enough was enough. The Mi-240 was the finest battle helicopter in the world, carrying a well-trained crew of six. It was time, they felt, to do what they had been trained to do: attack and destroy, and the hell with politics.

Denisov, flying far behind at the head of three more Mi-240s, heard the transmission.

"Contact those craft," he ordered the pilot, "and inform them that if they engage the train, I shall personally shoot the crews. They are not to destroy that train."

The two pilots heard the transmission but ignored it.

The country was changing from monotonous flatness to forested hills again, the rails running through deep cuts sliced in the hills. The train rattled through them, the engine noise echoing off the thick sides of the gouges in the mountainside. Above them on the slopes stood tall, silent pines.

As the train labored along the steep grades, Swanson and Wexler crawled out onto the flatcars and unhooked the couplings, leaving the rolling stock meandering along the rails to follow the locomotive at an ever decreasing rate. With the drag of the flatcars gone, the locomotive would pick up speed. It started hitting tunnels, roaring from the light into the darkness and into the light again.

Another hour passed, another fifty miles covered, before the two Mi-240s caught up with them.

"There they are," said the lead pilot.

"Stand by to engage."

The order thrilled both crews. They smelled blood in the air. Blood and victory.

The whine and thrust of the twin jet-assist engines that powered the two giant choppers split the afternoon air. The two death machines streaked through the sky at an immense speed. There was something about their bulk and the way they were handled that told the crew of the *Eagle* that these were machines piloted by ultraprofessionals. They would be hard to bring down. Maybe impossible. Instinctively, five sets of eyes settled on Milligan.

"Hey," he said, "don't look at me."

The Mi-240s came down for a look, flying at right angles across the track, darting by in a noisy flash.

The brief, perfunctory reconnaissance done, the Mi-240s closed for the kill. There would be no battle of skill with the machine guns this time. Two missiles fired at a very hot target that could take no evasive action would do the best—if least sporting—job. The two pilots expected the engagement to be over in a matter of minutes.

The lead helicopter swung down low and fired just as the engine pulled onto a curve. The rockets etched trails in the sky and flew over the cab so low that Milligan was sure he could have touched them as they passed overhead. The projectiles slammed into the mountainside. Rocks were thrown up, cascading down onto the tracks. The stately pines ballooned into bright flame.

"Christ!" someone screamed.

The engineer was jabbering away, begging the choppers in their own language to stop trying to kill him.

As the first chopper threw itself into a steep bank to come back for another pass, the other muscled itself into position. The bombardier was feeding new information into the aiming computer. The two missiles blasted off and struck the track just where the train had been seconds before. The explosion rocked the afternoon and tore up the railway ties, the force of the blast twisting the heavy steel rails like pipe cleaners.

They flashed into the darkness of the tunnel and Swanson jumped at the controls, doing what he had seen the driver do the last time they stopped. The driver jumped to help him. It had become obvious that the helicopters didn't give a damn about him. Better to be alive on the wrong side than dead on his own. The metal wheels screamed in protest as for the second time that day they had to grind themselves down on the rails. The gallery filled with a heavy, wet, hot pall of steam.

The train scraped along the tracks, metal wailing and shrieking, the tormented sound bouncing off the packed brick walls. It seemed as if the tunnel had suddenly become home to a thousand banshees. The bright white of the tunnel mouth got larger and larger as the train slid toward the opening. They all knew that the Mi-240s were waiting outside like cats standing sentry at a mouse hole. Let the train show itself and this time there would be no mistake.

Agonizingly slowly, the train slid to a halt. Drenched in sweat, the crew slumped against the cool metal walls. The steam in the tunnel condensed and settled on them like dew.

The sound of the choppers got loud and then louder, then diminished as they circled the mountainside, confident that their quarry couldn't escape this time.

FIFTEEN

"Jesus," said Wexler, laying his head against the side of the cab. "That was close. Too close."

The train chuffed, working like the lungs of a heavy smoker after a tough climb up a few dozen flights of stairs. A swirl of dust and gravel swept into the tunnel as one of the Mi-240s landed on the track at the mouth of the tunnel. A second later the sister ship touched down at the rear of the tunnel. The trap snapped shut, locking the crew of the Eagle in its cage.

"Well," observed Swanson, "I guess we're not riding out of here."

The choppers were shutting down, the big blades dipping down until they almost touched the ground.

"So now what?" asked Nasty. His leg didn't hurt as much now.

"It doesn't look like we're going to get rushed," said Marquez, heaving himself up to take a look down the tunnel.

"Not yet," said Smith.

There was a slight bend in the tunnel—enough of a curve to keep the train in the shadows. The engine and the men aboard blended in against the brick of the tunnel instead of being thrown into silhouette.

That was something at least. If a firefight broke out, at least they would be firing from the dark into the light. The Russians would have to look into the shadow for a target, whereas they, if they dared to enter the tunnel, would show outlines as sharp and distinct as targets on a firing range.

"They're not going to rush us until they have more men to use. What does an Mi-240 carry? Five, six men?"

"Six, I think," said Marquez.

"They could take us now," said Nasty.

"They don't dare," said Swanson. "They'll wait until the numbers are better."

"By which time," said Nasty, "I for one plan to be outa this rat hole."

"Frank," said Swanson, "I want you to get a gun and get close to the forward end of the tunnel. I want some sharpshooting. Stay low and see who you can get."

"You bet," said Milligan.

"Wex, you take the other end."

"Good hunting, Wex," said Milligan before he started down the tunnel.

"Hold it a minute," said Swanson. "Hang around and hear what else I've got lined up. We have to get out of here, right?"

"Right," chorused his men.

"We could rush one chopper and take it down, but by the

time we made it into the open the other one would be chewing on our ass.''

"Take 'em out together," said Marquez.

"Exactly," said Swanson.

"But how?" asked Smitty. "We don't have enough men."

"No, we don't. First, we get Wex and Frank to keep their heads down. The rest of us are going to get a head of steam up on the loco here, and when the time comes we'll set her moving."

"Which way?" asked Nasty.

"Backwards. Reverse it toward the bird behind us and hope those two pieces of machinery make an intimate acquaintance. The rest of us go forward and see what we can do up there."

"Listen," said Marquez, "I'd like—"

"Joe," said Swanson soberly, "you stay in the tunnel. You stay down and we'll come back and get you when the coast is clear."

Marquez leaned back against the tunnel wall. He didn't say anything.

"One problem, Major," said Milligan. "That forward chopper has a ball-mounted fifty-cal. When we come out of the tunnel, one of those fuckers could get to it and turn it on us. They can't get us now because we're in the bend of this tunnel. Once we're in the open, that gun'll make dog food out of a couple of us."

"Shit," said Swanson. He thought a moment. "Anyone got an answer to that one?"

"Besides blowing them away before they make a dash for the chopper?" asked Nasty.

"Yeah, besides that."

"Nope."

Marquez had a plan, but he kept his mouth shut.

"Then we just have to hope that we get lucky," said Swanson.

Milligan darted noiselessly through the tunnel, almost losing his footing twice on the slimy wooden ties between the rails. The crosspieces had been made slick by the constant dripping that dampened the interior of the tunnel.

It was an odd sensation, creeping through the black space like this. It was not unlike entering a movie theater after the feature has started. The open mouth of the tunnel—with a wide-open view of the chopper parked astride the tracks and the mountain landscape around and behind it—was as bright and clear as an image on a movie screen, while the darkness that Milligan was creeping through was as tangible and disorienting as the gloom of a theater.

He got as close to the front entrance as he dared and dropped down on his stomach. As he lay there he could hear the squawk and chatter of the radio the pilot had neglected to shut down. He brought the AK-47 up and swept the picture-window view with the barrel.

The crew had left the ship. They were hiding in a drainage ditch to the right of the track. Milligan's sharp eyes swept the margin of the track and saw what he wanted to see: a piece of an arm and a shoulder just sticking up.

"Ah," said Milligan. He wished he had a good sharp-shooting weapon—a Steyr or Mossberg would have done very nicely—because he wasn't looking at much of a target. It was something, but it wasn't much. If he missed, one of two things would happen: either the crew would crouch down lower and take care not to show an inch of themselves, or they would react and come up firing.

He licked his lips. If the crew jumped out of the ditch and started firing after he dropped the Russian he could see a piece of, Milligan was pretty sure he could take them all at once. He knew where they were; they would be firing wildly.

Carefully, he took aim. "Now c'mon out and play. . . ." he whispered.

Every member of the crew of the Mi-240 felt uncomfortable outside the protective cocoon of the potent helicopter. Crouched in their filthy ditch, they were aware of, but unable to see the yawning black maw of the tunnel; they felt like turtles stripped of their thick shells. But they had been ordered to keep the train bottled up inside the tunnel, and there had been only one way to do that—to land on the tracks. If they had circled or hovered they would have run dangerously low on fuel before reinforcements arrived.

The pilot was bored already and decided that there was nothing else he could do besides wait and think of something else. He rested his head on his forearm. His ear showed pink and clean over the edge of the ditch, like a wild flower growing in a hedgerow.

"Nice," whispered Milligan to himself. He fixed the ear in the protected post of the front sight and squeezed the trigger.

The bullets whippped a large chunk of the pilot's skull into the air like a cap swept off his head by a gust of wind. There was a scream from the ditch—not from the pilot; his fatal head wound had put him well past screaming—but from one of his horrified comrades, who found himself suddenly drenched in the brains of the dead man.

To Milligan's intense disappointment they didn't come leaping out from their cover. Instead, they cowered.

The tunnel grabbed the sounds of Milligan's firing and amplified and echoed them, throwing them from wall to wall. At the other end of the tunnel the crew of the second helicopter thought that the shooting meant something was happening; the Americans were foolishly trying to break out of their trap. With more guts than brains, two crew members jumped from their hiding place.

Wexler was waiting. He dropped them with a couple of well-placed shots before they managed to cover a yard.

Nasty, Swanson, and Smith ignored the fighting. They had their own job to do. They were working hard to shovel coal into the furnace, laboring frantically to stoke up the fires and get a good head of steam up before real trouble developed with the arrival of reinforcements.

Nobody was watching Marquez as he sat by the edge of the track, his back resting against the slimy wall of the tunnel. He felt stupid, helpless: the others had something to do, roles to perform, parts to play in this daring escape. He was just along for the ride now, slowing them down, narrowing further the already short odds on their escape. He decided to change that.

The men on the train were grunting over their exertions. Wexler and Milligan were hidden somewhere in the gloom of the tunnel. Marquez lurched to his feet, unsteady like a drunk, patted his pockets as if looking for something. Putting one hand against the slick wall to support himself, he started stumping down the tunnel toward Milligan's end.

Milligan didn't see Joe until he crossed the line between light and dark at the mouth of the tunnel. Marquez staggered into the brightness, holding his hand up.

"Surrender," he shouted. "I surrender." He waved his arms. "I give up."

"Marquez!" screamed Milligan. "Marquez, you son of a bitch! I carried you! Major!"

"Surrender," said Marquez, stumbling toward the Russians.

Swanson threw down his shovel and jumped from the footplate. Marquez had lost his mind.

"Joe! Joe!" His voice caromed off the walls.

"Marquez! You fuck!" shouted Frank Milligan. "You get back here or I'll . . ." He sighted the Kalashnikov between Marquez's shoulder blades.

At that moment Marquez reached into his pockets, grabbed his last two grenades, pulled the pins, and started to run. His leg seemed to burst into flame as he forced his tortured muscles to work. A Soviet airman had jumped out of the trench and tried to tackle Marquez. Joe dived into the open door of the Mi-240, the crew member right behind him.

Once inside, Marquez dropped the grenades, each clip snapping off its blasting cap. He smiled at his pursuer.

"So here we are," he said.

The giant helicopter exploded in a broiling sphere of flame. In a matter of seconds Marquez's act of self-destruction had started a devastating chain reaction. The grenades had detonated, tearing the cabin to shreds and starting a hot fire which superheated the hot tanks of aviation fuel in the tail of the craft. As these blew they ignited the remaining two air-to-air missiles lodged on the stubby wings of the helicopter fuselage. When they were done blowing, all that remained of the chopper was a smoking crater to mark the place where the Mi-240 had once been and a scatter of debris.

Swanson stopped and stared, transfixed by Marquez's suicide.

Milligan was screaming. "Goddammit! Goddammit!"

"Milligan," ordered Swanson, "get down!"

Nasty, back at the train, saw that the moment for the

attack had come. He shoved the Russian toward the short ladder. "Keep your head down, old man."

Smith unhooked the brakes and slammed the throttle around and set the gears for reverse. The train began groaning and then slowly started moving backward.

"Wex," yelled Nasty, "get the hell up here."

"You bet," said Wexler from the back end of the tunnel. When the rest of the *Eagle* force went through the front door of the tunnel, he wanted to be with them. He fired a couple of rounds at the concealed Russians just to keep them honest, then turned and ran.

As his footsteps clattered through the tunnel, a Russian jumped from his hiding place and darted a few yards to the mouth of the tunnel. He had a pistol in his hands. His shoulders hunched as he bent in the combat stance. He squeezed off four rounds.

Wexler felt as if he had been roughly pushed to the wet floor of the tunnel. It was only after he had lain dazed for a second beside the track that a nauseating wave of pain washed over him. He knew instantly what had happened. He'd been hit. Tears welled up in his eyes. It was the end of the road for him.

"Oh no, man," he muttered. As the locomotive rolled by him, rushing backward toward the other helicopter, he realized he couldn't feel his legs.

But the Russian airman's bullets had claimed another casualty. The driver of the train, hiding in the middle of the tunnel, had been hit in the back of the head by the fourth bullet. He had died without making a sound.

The blunt stern of the engine broke through the curtain of darkness and smashed into the heavy Mi-240, crushing the big ship like a bug. The air was suddenly heavy and intoxicating with the smell of aviation fuel. The two remaining crew members didn't have time to throw themselves flat before the sparks spurting from the smashed boiler of the train ignited the gas-rich air. It seemed like the day itself caught fire. A burst of flame as strong as a hurricane wind split the area around the mangled mixture of machinery. The locomotive and helicopter burned furiously. The ammunition on board the chopper started popping in the flames, sending bullets lashing into the wooded hillside. The missiles exploded with a thunderous boom, sending shock waves into the tunnel. Great hunks of masonry fell from the gallery ceiling. Smoke billowed, a tall column building in the fresh air.

At the other, front end of the tunnel, Milligan held the AK-47 at waist level and ripped a few rounds into the ditch. He jumped up onto the verge and looked down, his eyes smoldering.

But no one was left alive. The pilot, the first casualty, lay where Milligan had dropped him. The others were sprawled about, their bodies smashed by pieces of the first blown helicopter. One had been neatly decapitated. Blood flowed in the bottom of the trench as deep and as oily thick as stagnant water.

Milligan couldn't think of anything to say except, "All present and correct, sir."

"Where's Wex?" said Nasty.

They found him in the tunnel, dragging his dead legs behind him.

"The fuckers nailed me," he said, as if he had to explain.

There wasn't much blood, not on the outside anyway, but Wexler's abdomen was purple and mottled like a huge bruise. Two bullets had struck him near the kidney, another slightly to the left of the spine. You didn't have to be a doctor to know that there was spinal damage and internal bleeding.

"So what are you hanging around for?" demanded Wexler.

"Calm down," said Swanson. It was all he could say.

Wexler sighed. "I'm a mess. You know I can't travel. I'm gonna be dead soon, so why hang around?"

Swanson shook his head. "Listen, Wex . . ."

"Listen, nothing. Just put me in some cover, gimme a gun, and you guys hit the road."

"No," said Nasty.

Wexler laughed weakly. "What the fuck are you going to do, you big greaseball bastard? Operate?"

They carried him out into the light and awkwardly manhandled him up the slope a way and rested him between two boulders. He had a nice view of the tunnel mouth and the track from here.

"Gimme two clips off that nice Russian popgun and hit the trail."

"Wex," said Swanson, "I'm giving you an order. When they get here, you surrender."

"Or what? You'll have me court-martialed? Why are you hanging around?"

The four men stood around awkwardly, like family members at a deathbed.

"Please, guys," Wexler pleaded, "please. Go. Go home. I hope you make it. I know you will. I just won't be there to see it. That's it. Now go. . . ."

Milligan hugged his friend. "Bye, farmboy."

They slithered down the slope, tears streaming down their faces. They crossed the tracks and vanished into the forest on the far side. Wexler watched them go. He shifted his position slightly, almost crying out with the pain. "Bye, guys," he whispered.

He didn't have long to wait before the sound of choppers filled the air. He felt relaxed, like someone on a team that's going into a game while already knowing it has a place in the playoffs.

"Now to hold them off," he said to himself, "just like in the movies."

SIXTEEN

The sound of the chopper woke Swanson. He was nestled under a tall pine tree, sound asleep and dreaming of nothing. The sound of the helicopter broke through the shroud of sleep that enveloped him and jerked him awake. Smith, Nasty, and Milligan were awake too, straining to see the sky, hoping to catch a glimpse of the chopper.

They had run all night, trying to put as much distance as they could between themselves and the train tracks, but exhaustion had claimed them. By the time dawn was breaking they were stumbling along, scarcely able to raise a foot to take a step.

In the black of the night and now, in the bright light of afternoon, they had not been able to stop themselves from thinking about the costly engagement at the tunnel. In a matter of minutes they had lost two men.

But both were heroes. Both had given their lives that their

comrades might be spared. Both had died fighting, if not for their own freedom, then for the freedom of others. Theirs were glorious deaths, noble ones, but that didn't make it any easier for the living to accept their sacrifices.

When the chopper woke them, though, they all had the same thought: It's beginning again. They know where we are. Marquez and Wexler died in vain. . . .

The chopper came down low over the treetops, the whine of the engine and the wop-wop of the rotors so loud that the death machine seemed to know exactly where they were. But there was another sound mixed with the engine noise, a weird jangled sound that they listened to carefully for several passes of the aircraft before they realized it was heavily accented English that was pouring from the loud-speakers mounted on the underside of the helicopter.

"What the hell is that?" asked Milligan over the din.

"Probably just asking us to surrender," said Swanson. "Try not to listen."

"Listen?" said Nasty. "I can't hardly understand a word they're saying."

Then, as distinct and as hard as a diamond, they heard a word: Smith.

"Hey, Smitty," said Milligan, "you're being paged."

"What the hell is that all about?" asked Smith, puzzled.

But the chopper had passed on to the horizon. The helicopter was gone, but the word hung in the air. "They could still hear the heavily accented voice speaking the single word they had all understood: "Smeet."

"Don't worry about it, Smitty," said Swanson. "They always keep records of who flies our planes. We do the same thing for their guys. They probably just managed to find your file."

"Pretty strange, though," said Smith, shaking his head, "hearing your name in the sky like that."

"Forget it. Just pretend it was Tokyo Rose." They were wide awake now and hungry.

"Think we should risk a fire?" asked Nasty.

Swanson stared at the little patch of blue sky he could see between the trees. The sound of the chopper had passed out of earshot. The afternoon sounds of birds and the wind were the only signs that the world was alive that day.

Swanson weighed the problem carefully. His men had to eat. They needed a fire. They had to stay alive. What were the chances a fire could be seen from the air? Russia was a big country.

"Let's have a fire," said Swanson.

"Great," said Nasty. "What are we going to eat?"

"Beets," said Swanson, "that's all there is."

"Beets," said Nasty, "I love 'em."

They boiled the water and ate the beets. They were gray and tasteless, but warm and filling.

"I always thought beets were red," said Nasty. "I could never stand that red color."

"SAC knew that," said Milligan. "They made them gray like this just to keep you guessing."

"Let's move it," said Swanson.

Nasty checked their position and they moved off. The going was tough. They labored up and down hillsides and fought their way through underbrush, forded streams, clambered over rocks. It got harder once the sun went down. Blinded by the darkness, they stumbled and cursed and got weaker. By midnight they were exhausted again.

Swanson called a halt at a clearing. Near a stream there was a natural bed of grass that was so soft and short it looked like a front lawn lovingly tended by suburbanites.

They lay down and were asleep in a matter of seconds—all of them, that was, except Arnie Smith. He lay awake for as long as he could, running the weird announcement through his analytical mathematician's brain. They had his name. What did that mean? Why were they calling for him? It made him feel uneasy. They knew him. They knew about him. He fell into a sleep filled with disquiet and disjointed dreams of trains and conifers and giant loudspeakers from which his name blasted in bad English.

Denisov would dearly have liked to have gone to bed himself. But before he could do so, the major had summoned him from his tiny room in the command post and informed him that he had a visitor.

"Who is it?" asked Denisov irritably. He had had a very bad day. Three helicopters lost, and a lone American had held up the advance of the reinforcements for two and a half hours by sniping from behind a pile of rocks. He had killed six men before being killed himself. The American's nerve seemed to have known no bounds. He had refused to surrender, had been stunningly accurate, and had been killed only after he had run out of ammunition. When they shot him—the fools, they had orders to take all of them alive—he had been trying without success to push a boulder down the hill on top of them. This had been Wexler, a man about whom Denisov knew very little. If they were all like him, if they fought with such single-mindedness . . .

Denisov began to have the tiniest feeling of doubt. Could it be possible that the remaining members of Swanson's little band would escape? He clenched his fist. No. Absolutely not. They could not possibly get away. He told himself that before the next day came to an end he would have captured Smith. Once he had one of them, he would have them all.

But would he?

"A visitor?" he said to the major. "Who?"

"A gentleman from Moscow," said the major with a smirk. "A gentleman from Dzerzhinsky Square."

"Ah," said Denisov. He wondered if he was going to be relieved of his command. "I will come at once."

The KGB man sat behind Denisov's uncle's desk, drinking his uncle's cognac. The general was nowhere to be seen. Denisov entered and looked with distaste at the very fat, pig-eyed man with the thick lips and the double chin.

The KGB man looked back at the colonel with equal disdain. He hated people like Denisov, so self-assured, so convinced of their own semidivinity. Denisov had, by luck of birth, been born into a powerful family, had powerful friends, and was used to the best of everything from the West. He didn't appreciate what he had; he expected it. Men like Denisov sniggered up their sleeves at people like him, a back-street brawler who had risen to his present position by ruthlessly shooting the men he was told to shoot, torturing men he was ordered to torture.

Denisov was used to being deferred to, even protected. That was going to change right now, and the man from the KGB was going to enjoy changing the colonel's charmed life.

He got straight to the point. "You're doing a shit job of this thing, Denisov. You are completely incompetent. Almost a moron, I would say."

Denisov was unmoved. "May I ask who you are?"

"Shut up, you little prick. Where are the fliers? These Americans."

"I'm looking for them."

"Oh, you are? I was concerned that you had forgotten."

"I have not forgotten."

"Shut up. I have been sent to oversee you. Now you have a partner. Together we shall find this scum."

Denisov tensed. In his short and glorious career he had

never once been treated this way. His luck was changing for the worse. For the first time in his life he was worried. It was a most disagreeable sensation.

"What is your name?"

"Szymanski."

"Rank?"

"Higher than yours. Now tell me how you are going to find these bastard Americans."

"I'm going to spring a trap."

Traps were something Szymanski understood, if they weren't too complicated. Faking it so someone looked like a fag, that was one of his favorite traps, but he didn't see how it could have worked here.

"What's the bait?"

"A little old lady," said Denisov.

Almost a week after the battle at the tunnel, they had stopped in midafternoon to soak their feet in a cold stream that tumbled down among the pines.

"Ah," said Nasty, "that feels good."

"Yeah," agreed Swanson.

"Listen," said Milligan, "choppers."

Sure enough, from far off came the flapping sound they had come to loathe.

"Damn," said Nasty, pulling his burning feet from the cool water. "Just when I was starting to enjoy myself."

They sprinted over the pine-needle floor to the cover of some trees and lay flat, waiting for the chopper to go over. The closer it got to them, the more they realized that it was playing that tape again, louder this time, more distinct.

"Lieutenant Smith, United States Strategic Air Command . . ." The chopper was very close now, the sound from the loudspeaker so intense that it distorted, warping the words.

But this time they got enough of the message to know exactly what the Russians were talking about. By the time the chopper had passed on, blaring its message into the wilderness, Smith was white-faced and shaken.

"Don't even think about it," said Swanson. "It's gotta be a trap."

"Those rat bastards," hissed Nasty. "That is dirty pool."

"*Fuckin'* dirty pool," put in Milligan. "Using an old lady like that. We're kicking their goddamn asses, so they have to pull this kind of shit to beat us."

The announcement from the helicopter had been blunt. The KGB knew of Smith's Russian ancestry. They had located a member of his mother's family, an elderly woman. If Smith did not give himself up, the woman would be shot.

Smith exhaled heavily. "This is a tough one. . . ."

"No, it isn't," said Swanson shortly. "It's not a tough one. It's easy. You ignore it."

"C'mon, Captain, how can I? Maybe it's a put-up, but maybe it isn't. If it isn't, I figure that they wouldn't think twice about killing some old lady. Remember, I come from a Jewish family. As far as these guys are concerned it would just be one less . . ."

"Now think, Arnie, did you mother or father ever talk about family they had left behind here?"

Smith nodded unhappily. "Yeah, all the time. When birthdays would roll around or me or my sister would graduate from high school or something, my mother would say, I wish your grandmother or your aunt or somebody could be around to see this."

"So you do have family here."

Smith nodded.

"Well, I'm afraid that's just tough for them, Arnie. I am not allowing you to give yourself up. That's final. Forget it.

And you can take that as an order. Now, seems to me like we've wasted enough time already. Let's get moving."

The country was very rugged now, the forests thicker, the hills steeper. Although it was tough going, there was a good side to it as well. Swanson sensed that with every step they took deeper into the forests they were becoming harder and harder to find. Large numbers of searchers were useless in this kind of terrain. Choppers would have a hard time finding them, and even if they did there were few places they could land.

Nasty climbed a tree as soon as it was dark, heaving himself high up into the branches to get a good look at the night sky. It was an odd position to compute their position from, but he enjoyed it. High up above the ground, in the middle of the silent pines, he could look out and see the forest gleaming beneath the newly risen moon. It was a peaceful and oddly reassuring sight.

He climbed down with a grin on his face. He wanted to check his figures with Smith, but he had a feeling he was dead right. Smith concurred.

Nasty cleared his throat and, as if he were a juror announcing the verdict after a long and complicated trail, said: "Gentlemen, the voo for today says that we have traveled one thousand five hundred and nineteen miles. We, your highly skilled navigators, are pleased to inform you that we are now one hundred miles from the coastal town of Anadyr."

Swanson and Milligan clapped. But they couldn't help but feel sad. It had been a week since the engagement at the train tunnel. If only Marquez and Wexler had been able to be with them, they would have been happy.

The chopper made one more visit. They had heard it dozens of times now, so often that they had stopped looking for it, stopped listening to the announcement—all of them, that was, except Smith.

Actually, they could never be sure that it was the same chopper. There must have been dozens out looking for them, and the fact that it passed over them so often suggested that they didn't have anything more than a general idea of where they were. If there were soldiers in the woods, then they never saw them.

That night, however, the chopper's monotonous message was slightly different. They had given Smith's aunt a name: Lydia Feodorovna Berg.

"Ignore it, Arnie."

"Yeah," said Smith, "right."

When they awoke in the morning, he was gone.

SEVENTEEN

Denisov put down his telephone and turned to his new colleague.

"They have Smith."

"Took long enough," growled Szymanski. "Where is he?"

"They have taken him to Anadyr."

"Get your hat, pretty boy. That's where we are going."

The major smiled. It was his lucky day. Denisov was finally leaving the command post and this pig from the KGB was making the cocky colonel's life unbearable. What more could the major ask for?

Smith had stolen away from the camp in the dead of night, shivering in the darkness. He left everything he had carried all this way. Freed of his pack and his weapons, he made good time and he had little difficulty finding his way with the only piece of equipment he had taken with him: his compass. They had all been issued one, so his would not be missed.

He felt bad that he couldn't say good-bye to the remaining members of the crew of the *Eagle*, but he knew that if he had tried Swanson would never have let him go. He felt sad to leave only because they had come so far and done so much together as a team. Leaving without thanking them or telling them that they were the best and that he had been proud to serve with them made him feel empty.

But he had to go. He had to make sure that some innocent old lady didn't suffer on his behalf. If he hadn't gone it would have lain heavy on his conscience for the rest of his life. He wondered if the Russians would abide by the terms of the Geneva Conventions covering prisoners of war. He thought of the choppers shot down, the soldiers they had killed, the chaos they had created. He thought of the band of misguided kids they had decimated and knew in his bones he wasn't going to see any mercy from his captors.

Once having decided to be captured, Smith encountered a great deal of trouble actually giving himself up. The Russians seemed to be lost. He walked all day looking for a patrol or a chopper but found nothing. He was hungry, but it didn't matter much anymore. When he found a clearing near a stream—had they camped here once themselves?—he decided to sit out the night there, making himself a big fire and hoping it would be seen from the air. It wasn't.

He fell into an uneasy sleep but awoke in the morning to the sound of a helicopter. He felt something like relief when he stepped into the warm sunlight of the clearing, showing himself plainly to his pursuers.

They took him to a scrubby-looking little town not much different from the one where they had stolen the train days before. The helicopter crew looked curiously at him as they ferried him over the forests and down to the sea, but Smith had not been mistreated. They gave him a seat behind the pilot and a crewman sat next to him, holding a gun in his meaty hand. Surrounded by these healthy, well-fed men, Smith suddenly realized the extent of the privations he had suffered during the long trek. He was gaunt, weak, and dirty. His clothes hung on his body like tattered sails. His guns bled from lack of nutrition.

He was only spoken to once. Just as the chopper came in for a landing at a town beside the silver-gray sea, the pilot pointed east and said one word: "America."

Smith nodded. That was the way home to a land he would never see again. He was going to be buried in the land of his fathers and their fathers, a land which had oppressed them, murdered them, and finally scorned them. A land that his own parents had turned their back upon. And now, after they had found freedom in their new land, the cycle had come full circle—their son would again be imprisoned in the old. A strange fate for a quiet kid from Chicago who wanted to get a Ph.D. in mathematics.

He had been taken to a cell and left there. It had not been the foul dungeon he expected. Rather, it was simply a small cement-walled room with a cot to sleep on and bucket in the corner. A single light bulb was set in a little cage high up on the wall and recessed into the concrete. There was no window. He was pushed inside and the light was snapped off. He lay down on the bed and slept a peaceful sleep.

The light came on and woke him up. Then came the rattling of a key in the heavy steel door. His watch had been taken away from him when he arrived at the prison, so he had no idea how long he had slept. He had the impression it was late at night.

Two soldiers entered and told him to stand up. He did so. They led him down the narrow corridor a short distance to another room not much larger than his cell. It was furnished only with a heavy wooden chair—it reminded him of an electric chair—with thick leather straps on the arms and leg.

"Sit," said the guard. He sat.

He waited a long time, growing more nervous with the passage of each minute. A single chilling detail caught his eye. There was a drain in the middle of the floor of the room next to the chair. The floor had been sloped so liquid would run off easily.

The door opened and two men entered. One was heavy and thick faced. In his stubby fingers he held a cigarette. The other was thin and wore a well-cut uniform. He too was smoking. They said nothing—nothing to him, nothing to each other.

The big, stupid-looking one walked straight up to Smith and without warning jammed the cigarette out on his cheekbone. As the red-hot tip of the cigarette seared his flesh, Smith screamed and bucked in the chair. He had not yet been manacled so he grabbed at the big man's hands and tried to wrench them away, but Szymanski caught Smith's weak arms and thrust them aside. The cigarette crumbled in his fingers and he stepped back like an artist admiring his handiwork.

The burn had blistered immediately, leaving an angry red crater on the peak of Smith's cheekbone. It felt like his face was on fire. Two soldiers entered and bound Smith to the chair. As they were working the big man said something to the thin one. Denisov translated:

"The gentleman says that he did that just to get your attention."

From between clenched teeth Smith said, "He got it."

"Good. Please tell me where your comrades are."

Smith said nothing. He didn't even look at the man. He tried to control the panic rising within him.

"Please, Lieutenant Smith. It will be very painful for you

otherwise. . . ." The big man advanced menacingly a step.

"You and your comrades have performed brilliantly. You have proven your point. There is no reason to go on. You have come here of your own free will. Please cooperate."

"I came to save the life of a relative."

Denisov smiled. In that moment Smith knew he had been tricked. There was no aunt. There was no Lydia Feodorovna.

"Please, Lieutenant Smith. I don't think I have to tell you that this is not a pleasant man." He gestured at Szymanski.

As if to prove Denisov's assertion, the KGB man stepped forward and punched Smith hard, full in the mouth. His lips mashed against his teeth; he felt two teeth crack and split, chips of enamel filling his mouth like grit. Blood poured from his mouth, dribbling down the front of his torn flight suit.

"How do you expect him to speak with his mouth like that, you ignoramus," said Denisov petulantly.

"Shut up," said Szymanski, hitting Smith again. It was in the eye this time. The delicate skin on the eyebrow split over the bone and more blood flowed. Smith quite literally saw stars. The blow had pulled at the burn, causing him pain from two places. In a matter of minutes he had been horribly disfigured.

"I cannot tell you anything," he said through broken lips and teeth.

"Tell me where they are going. Where are they going?"

Smith fought to wipe his mind free of any information. He couldn't tell them anything. He couldn't allow himself to give away his buddies.

"Lieutenant Smith," said Denisov despairingly, "please, I beg you, do not be so foolish."

"Shut up, Denisov," growled Szymanski. "You've had your chance. My turn now."

The KGB man pushed back his sleeves and waded into Smith. As he advanced he looked like a fat man about to sit down to a hearty dinner.

Arnold Smith couldn't fathom how long the torture lasted. It must have been quite awhile. He was beaten, doused with ice-cold water, beaten, and doused again. His clothes were stripped off his body and shocks belted through him. Through it all he screamed. Screamed so loud that he was sure he would scream his voice box out of his throat. Through it all Szymanski growled and cursed and muttered. Denisov left the room, not because he was sickened by the violence—he had seen it many times before, and indeed, he did think torture had a role to play in these matters. What had turned his stomach was how much Szymanski seemed to enjoy it.

Then it had stopped. He had been dragged back to his dark cell and thrown on the bed. His mind and body were a mass of pain and fear, a furious storm of terror and torment.

The pain was incredible, but he tried to harness it, to use it to clear his mind. His fear was born not of what they would do to him next—what more could they do? how much more painful could it become?—rather, he was scared of letting go. He was scared of talking. He wasn't sure he could prevent his mind from suddenly releasing the information that was stored in it. He knew that he would tell them they were headed for Anadyr. That they would try and find a boat, that they would try and sail to Attu or Agattu. If he said that, they would be waiting for them. They would die and it would be his fault. He knew they would die— Swanson, Milligan, and Nasty would not allow themselves to be taken alive.

The solution was simple. He had to die. He had to kill

himself, right then in the dark little cell. He couldn't see anything in the blackness, but he summoned up an image of the room. A bed, a bucket, a light. A germ of an idea formed in his mind. If he could get to the light, he could break the bulb and cut his wrists. It was not the most effective form of suicide, but it was all he could do. He was about to put his plan into action when the key rattled in the lock.

"Oh, God," he said, "please. Please not now. . . ."

A guard bustled into the room and put something down on the floor. It was metal and heavy and Smith heard it scrape on the cold concrete.

"Water," said the guard.

After he had gone, Smith gingerly lifted himself off the bed and, aching from every part of his body, felt his way to the bucket. The water was cool against his brow. He dribbled a little of the liquid past his split lips. It stung but it felt good too.

Now it was time to get to work. He groped his way back to the bed and slowly stood upright. He was as crook-backed as an old man and he hurt all over. The extension of his body required to reach the light fixture caused him even greater pain, but he had to do it. His fingers felt the wire cage around the light bulb and found that it was slightly loose where it had been screwed into the wall. Four screws secured it, one at each corner.

During his weeks on the run his fingernails had grown thick and long. Those were the only tools he had to work with. Very carefully, he found the groove in a screw, inserted his thumbnail, and worked at the tough little piece of metal.

An hour later he was still working on the first screw. Several times he had had to sit down to rest his broken body. His fingernails were broken and split, the skin on the ends of his fingers bleeding and raw. He couldn't get the screws to move.

Almost weeping with frustration he sat down on the edge of the bed and tried to think. All he needed was something hard and thin edged—a coin, a sliver of metal, it didn't matter what. But he was blind and naked in a room with two objects. He ran his fingers over every inch of the bed and found nothing that he could use. The entire structure had been welded together, leaving not the slightest bit of protruding metal that he could adapt to his needs.

Then he found it. As he had been working and thinking, he had unconsciously been worrying one of the broken teeth in his jaw with his tongue. His tongue had rocked it back and forth the way he had done when he was kid waiting for his second teeth to grow in. In a flash he realized that the loose, dead tooth was just what he needed. He seized it between his thumb and forefinger, almost gagging as he forced his fist into his mouth. A couple of rocks back and forth and the incisor came away from his jaw without pain. He held the tooth in his hand as if it were a diamond.

He climbed back up to the grid and with movements as careful and as delicate as he could manage he slid the tooth into the groove of the screw. Working with the tiny end that protruded from the slot, he twisted his wrist, trembling with the effort to stay calm.

He almost shouted for joy when he felt the screw give a fraction of an inch. It took him forty minutes to remove the first screw. At the end of two hours he had succeeded in removing three. He didn't bother with the last one. Using that as a hinge, he swung the grid away from the light bulb.

Very carefully and almost laughing with joy, he unscrewed the light bulb. Holding it in one hand, he felt his way down the wall and maneuvered himself into a sitting position on the edge of the bed. He was going to break the bulb on the edge of the bed but misjudged the force of the blow.

He had meant to tap the bulb on the frame, breaking it as one would an egg, but he hit it too hard. The bulb exploded in a million minute slivers, not one of them large enough to slit his wrists.

He threw himself back on the bed and wept.

Then he realized that there were sounds in the corridor. It was an argument; the two men who had tortured him were coming again, wrangling about who was going to be accorded the privilege of killing him, of finishing him off.

Panic gave him the plan that would kill him. Suddenly he saw it clearly. He knew exactly what he would do. He bent down and picked up the bucket of water, slopping the liquid as he lifted it up. He placed it on the bed and stuck his bloody, dirty foot in the cool water.

The voices were getting louder. Smith could hear the jangling keys of the jailer.

He jammed his fingers into the empty light socket and hung from it.

The lock was thrust into the door. Smith heard the door swing on its hinges.

"Come," said a guard gruffly. He snapped on the light.

There was a spark and a flash. Smith's body went rigid and his mouth opened in a silent scream. There was a smell of burning flesh and hair. The powerful jolt of electricity stopped his brave heart midbeat.

EIGHTEEN

They had found the sea. When they broke out of the forest onto the scrubby coastal plain, they had smelled it. They stopped dead in their tracks and drank in the air, trying to catch the rich, salty smell in their lungs. It smelled like freedom.

Swanson thought back to his daydream, the mental image he carried like a sacred icon of Sammy on the beach that day at Point Reyes. The smell had been the same. It was the same ocean. But he had to fight to prevent himself from thinking they were almost home. Because they weren't even close.

Another hour's march and they found themselves on a steep cliff overlooking the gray, cold ocean, the choppy, treacherous thoroughfare that they had to cross before they could claim victory. It stretched away to the horizon.

"I dunno," said Milligan, speaking for all of them. "I somehow figured we'd be able to see the islands."

He was right. They had expected to see the ragged-edged archipelago of the Aleutians stretched out before them. But all they saw was water. It could have been the Pacific at its widest.

"Sure this is the right place?" asked Milligan.

"Have I steered you wrong yet?" retorted Nasty huffily.

"Always a first time," said Milligan.

"How far are we from Anadyr?" asked Swanson.

"Thirty, forty clicks maybe," said Nasty.

Swanson had known for the last few days that they were going to have to change their plans. Originally they had hoped they could steal a boat from a coastal town. Now, though, the way they looked and felt from the trek, they could no more take on a town than they could a Soviet battalion.

"So which way?" asked Milligan.

"That way," said Nasty, pointing southwest.

"So let's go."

"Hold it a minute," said Swanson. "I have to figure something out."

They sat under a misshapen pine tree that looked as if it had been twisted by a disease. In fact, the buffeting of the cruel wind day in and day out had turned the old tree in on itself.

"I'm going down to the beach," said Milligan, walking away toward the cliff side.

Nasty stretched out on his back and closed his eyes. it was cold and his blanket was in shreds.

"Not exactly a vacation spot, is it?" he said.

Swanson tried to think, but no plan would come to him. It was intensely frustrating to have come so far, to have fought so hard and labored so long to get where they were now and find that they were trapped, not by men but by geography.

The sound of the chopper pulled him from his thoughts. Nasty's eyes snapped open.

"Take cover," said Swanson.

"We're under all the cover there is in this neighborhood."

The two big men jammed themselves up against the stunted tree and, in the absence of anything else they could do, prayed that the chopper didn't see them.

The helicopter appeared like an insect on the horizon. It was coming in low and slow, lazily combing the headlands and beach for signs of the Americans. It seemed to take an hour rather than five minutes to come into view and then to fly out of sight again.

Eventually it disappeared over the horizon and the two men relaxed.

"Didn't see us," said Nasty with relief.

"Or Milligan."

"Where the hell is he anyway?"

Milligan clambered up from the beach a few minutes later. He stood over his two companions, his pack dripping wet and gritty with gray sand and seaweed.

"Did you see how low that fuckin' thing was? Low and slow, that's how I like them. I wish there was some way we cold shoot one down just a little bit. You know what I mean. I wouldn't mind a chopper ride home."

"Sure would be nice," said Nasty.

"By the way," said Milligan, upending his sack. Oysters tumbled out onto the sandy soil. "Lunch is served."

The shellfish were delicious. Milligan pried them open with a dexterity that amazed Nasty and Swanson, although they should have been used to Milligan's tricks by now.

"Where the hell did you learn to do that?" said Nasty.

"The Beachcomber Bar, Wellfleet Mass," said Milligan, his tongue working an oyster out of its shell. "I used to work at the raw bar outside. Every summer, from the time I was fifteen till I was eighteen. I used to serve the rich kids oysters while they sat in the sun and drank beer and talked about how an Audi was better than a BMW. I used to have to ring this stupid ship's bell if someone tipped me a dollar. It sucked, that job. Great bar, though. Me and my buddies could drink there like normal people when we weren't—"

"Chopper!" said Swanson.

"Fuck!" said Milligan. The three of them didn't fit under the tree, but this time the chopper was going faster. It flashed over them in a matter of seconds without a backward glance.

"Jeez," said Nasty, "this place is getting awfully popular."

"Regular patrols," said Swanson. "They must have guessed our rate of travel and figured that we'd be heading for the sea. If I'm right, I'd guess that there's a pretty heavy band of soldiers behind us somewhere, trying to flush us out, pushing us up against the sea. The choppers will keep flying back and forth looking for us."

"Not if we blast 'em out of the sky," said Milligan.

"There'll just be another one after it," said Nasty soberly. "I guess this means we're not going to go look for a boat. If we take one step toward the town, this Anadyr place, then they're going to jump on our asses."

"Yeah," said Swanson, "that's about the size of it."

They were silent for a while.

Finally Swanson looked up. "Anyone got any ideas? 'Cause if you don't, I have one that has absolutely no chance of succeeding."

"We're all ears," said Nasty.

When Swanson finished, even Milligan looked doubtful. "I was just kidding, you know, when I said that we could just shoot one down a little."

"Seems to me like there's nothing else we can do."

Milligan shrugged. "It's going to mean some pretty good shooting."

"You can handle it, Frank."

"I appreciate your confidence," said Milligan, "but one mistake and we're screwed."

"Simple," said Nasty. "Don't fuck up."

They had about a two-hour wait for the next chopper. While they waited they went through the plan again.

At the first sound of the helicopter, Nasty and Swanson would leave their cover and Nasty would stretch out on the ground in plain sight as if he were badly hurt. Swanson would wave the chopper in, as if in surrender, doing his best to act broken, defeated, and submissive. It was his guess that the helicopter would hover for a while, taking a closer look and reporting to headquarters. In all probability it would get the okay to land.

At that point Milligan had to do the best shooting of his life. His target would be the pilot and co-pilot and they had to be taken out with split-second timing and letter-perfect accuracy. The choppers that had been patrolling were not the heavily armed, heavily manned Mi-240s but lighter, less well-equipped machines. If there were more than two crew members to each copter, then the three men hadn't seen them. In order for the plan to work there had to be only two men aboard.

Once the chopper had settled and the controllers had been greased, Swanson had to get into the cockpit and in control before the whole thing flipped over. A running helicopter with no firm hand at the control was a dangerously unpredictable beast. If they got hold of the machine, they were home free.

If not, they were done for. Swanson figured that the pilot would radio his position as soon as he saw them. Every chopper in the area would be speeding to the scene. If they didn't take off immediately, if they lost control of the helicopter, or even if it didn't land to pick them up, then they would be caught. There would be no running away this time. There was no place left to run.

Their hearts were pounding as the copter whirled into view. They had made a little blind for Milligan. He was pretty well concealed, but if someone was looking for him, he could be spotted. Swanson was counting on the pilot and co-pilot staring at one spot.

The chopper flew right over them and then continued on its way down the coast. They hadn't even been noticed.

"Son of a bitch!" said Nasty. "What are they, fuckin' blind? What do they want? An invi-fuckin'-tation?"

As he spoke the chopper wheeled in the sky and came back. The pilot thought he might have seen something.

The bubble snout of the machine buzzed toward them. The co-pilot was already busy raising his control on the radio.

"We have a sighting. We have a sighting. There are two men on the cliffs. I repeat, two men." He found it hard to keep the excitement from his voice. From behind the cockpit the gunner leaned forward.

"Should I shoot them?"

"Don't be so damned trigger-happy," growled the pilot into his throat mike.

"Anadyr control to unit six. Restate, please."

"We are thirty-one kilometers north of control," explained the co-pilot. "We have two of the Americans in sight. One appears to be hurt, the other is waving his arms. He's bringing us down."

"Instructions, please, Anadyr," said the pilot.

"Maintain visual contact with the enemy," was the reply.

"Fuck," hissed Nasty without moving his lips. "The mother fucker is hovering."

Denisov had been called. He dashed into the radio room and grabbed the microphone. "This is Denisov. I want them alive. Do you hear me? Alive."

The pilot looked around at his gunner. "Sorry, Shorty."

"Shall we apprehend, control?" asked the co-pilot.

Denisov thought a moment. "Yes. Go in. But go in with extreme caution. I do not want this mission ruined by your incompetence."

The crew of the chopper exchanged disgusted glances. "Charming fellow," said the pilot. He eased the cyclic lever up and the chopper lost a few feet.

"They're coming in, Nasty," whispered Swanson.

"Fantastic," said Nasty.

"Just for the hell of it," the pilot said to the gunner, "have your weapon ready."

The gunner grinned and cocked his machine gun.

The chopper dropped a few more feet and the men on the ground could feel the wind thrown down by the powerful rotors.

"Let's be nice and calm now," said the pilot.

"No incompetence," laughed the co-pilot.

The chopper lost a few more feet. They were about thirty-five feet up now and all were staring down at Swanson and Nasty. Sand and brush were floating up from the cliff. Swanson squinted against it, wiping grit from his eyes with one as he made a surrendering motion with the other.

The blow-back from the rotors had completely stripped Milligan of his cover. He was still lying flat, the nose of the AK-47 pointed into the swirling dust.

As the first skid hit the ground, the pilot cut his speed way down. The dust cloud was considerably reduced. Like the clouds parting on an overcast day to reveal a brilliant sun, the airborne debris vanished and Milligan had a clear shot at the pilot. He saw that he was jabbering into his headset, giving a blow-by-blow account of the capture of the two Americans.

Denisov listened to the flat, deadpan tones of the pilot and found himself tensing up, as if a wire were being wound tighter and tighter within him. If the Americans escaped now . . . He hated to think of the consequences.

Swanson had crouched low on the ground to avoid the rotors. He looked as if he were kneeling before his captors. At least that's what the pilot thought he was doing.

"He's kneeling down!" he reported, his voice suddenly jubilant. "He has totally surrendered."

Denisov knew the man was Swanson. He also knew that Swanson would kneel to no one.

Denisov lunged for the microphone, tearing it from the operator's hands.

"It's a trick!" he shrieked.

At that moment Milligan shot the pilot. Less than half a second later, the co-pilot was dead.

The gunner kicked open the door and fired. He hadn't seen Milligan, and Swanson was already sprinting for the far side of the helicopter, the pilot's side. The gunner only had one target left.

He shot Nasty as he rose from the ground to help secure the craft.

Swanson tore open the door on the pilot side. The gunner swung around with his machine gun to take out the other American. He never saw the Colt in Swanson's hand. He heard the shot but never felt the wound.

The cockpit was filled with smoke and the smell of cordite. Swanson wrestled with the straps that held the dead pilot in his seat. He unsnapped them and yanked the dead weight of the man out onto the grass. The man's foot caught in the rudder pedal and the chopper gave a sickening lurch to starboard. Swanson dove into the seat and fumbled with the unfamiliar controls, desperate to find the throttle. He had to get the speed down or the unstable machine would hop up, then over.

As he wrestled with the controls, he looked through the shattered canopy and saw Milligan kneeling over Nasty. He was resting his head on his chest.

Swanson's hands closed over the throttle and brought the machine down to a manageable level of revs. He leaned over, unbuckled the co-pilot, and kicked him out of the open door. The gunner he left where he was.

Milligan looked squarely at Nasty.

"You son of a bitch, you did not come all this way, put us through so much trouble about beets to die now."

Tears streamed down his face.

"Cut me a break, will you, Frank?" said Nasty weakly.

"No fuckin' way." He heaved Nasty over his shoulder and carried him to the chopper. He pulled the gunner from the rear of the craft and pitched him headlong onto the ground. He laid Nasty in his place and then threw himself down in the co-pilot's seat.

"You wanna get us the fuck home, Major? Would you do that?" said Milligan.

Jerkily, unsteadily, the chopper lifted into the sky.

NINETEEN

Denisov had listened with horror to the sound of a shot followed by an impenetrable wall of static. He had looked around the room at the other operators, the duty officers, and the clerks. All work had come to a stop. They were all looking at him. They were frozen at their tasks, the burbling and hiss of routine transmissions coming through unattended sets.

Szymanksi had stepped forward, roughly elbowing Denisov aside. "I am in command of this operation," he blustered. "I want all flying units to converge on the last location of unit six. Ground troops are to—"

"No," whispered Denisov, "they should not go to where the helicopter was. They must go where it's going." He spoke as if he were explaining some very basic problem to a child. It was a tone of voice well-known and feared in the old days, the glory days, when Denisov was the brightest officer in the Red Army.

"We do not know that the helicopter has left," said Szymanski.

"It has left. They are gone."

"Shut up." He swung around to look at everyone else in the room. "I gave an order. Get working! Do I have to draw you a picture?"

The clerks and operators went back to their machines and the duty officers bustled about. They hadn't liked Denisov, but this oaf from the KGB . . . They fervently hoped that he wouldn't be with them too long.

Their blood ran cold when Szymanski said, "Don't go anywhere, Denisov. You are, of course, under arrest."

Denisov shrugged. "Of course." He didn't seem to care anymore.

The chopper went out low as fast as Swanson dared take the unfamiliar ship. The controls were labeled in Russian, of course, and there was a heart-stopping moment when he reached to open a fuel tank and found himself in a stall that seemed to last a lifetime. The ship had pitched heavily and he had to fight it back to something like level flying. As the chopper rocked, Nasty shifted on his seat and groaned in pain.

"You want to keep it steady, Major?" snapped Milligan.

"How is he?"

"He was fuckin' fine until you slid him all over the sky." He leaned back over his friend. "It's okay, Nasty, man. It's good. It's cool. We're almost home. U.S.A. We got ourselves this beautiful chopper and we're just gonna fly ourselves home. Got it? So don't you go dying on me, you Guinea bastard. Don't even think about it."

Milligan choked back tears. Swanson knew what was

happening. Frank Milligan had been so strong for so long, but now his tortured psyche couldn't take a minute more strain. The shock of seeing his friend seriously wounded so close to victory had hurt him badly. It was best, Swanson thought, to let him get it all out, all the force of stress, the shock and horror of seeing another good man cut down.

The trouble was, Swanson didn't know where they were. There was no land beneath them and the light was failing. He figured that if he kept up the speed and maintained a course more or less due east, he would eventually hit American territory. If he had to deviate from that course, he would find himself lost and running low on fuel. His eyes swept the cockpit for the fuel gauges and found what he thought were the correct set of dials.

He frowned as he read them. He wondered how much fuel these things burned. He cursed himself for not having refreshed his knowledge about choppers sometime before the war. But he had never foreseen himself being in this position.

Behind him a battle fleet was building. Szymanski had ordered anything that could fly into the sky. He was in charge now and he would not fail like Denisov. When this mission was over, he would be covered with glory. No one was going to arrest him.

The Soviet choppers assembled as ordered at the last reported position of unit six of the coastal patrol. There, as Denisov had predicted, searchers found three bodies, some oyster shells, and an IGA coach gun, which Milligan had left behind. The flight commander took the last as a souvenir.

Orders came in from Szymanski. The patrol was to proceed out to sea. But valuable time had been lost, so the commanders had to increase their speed to catch up—their flying time would be limited. With predictable heavy-handedness Szymanski insisted that *all* the choppers set out in search of Swanson and his dwindling party instead of ordering some out and bringing others back to refuel and set out later to take over from their comrades.

That simple mistake gave Swanson a chance.

But he didn't know that. The radar scope aboard his ship picked up the massed choppers as they zeroed in on him. The number of blips on the scope was ominously large.

"Holy shit," he whispered. "Frank . . ."

"Yeah?"

"We got trouble."

"Well, we oughta be used to that by now." Milligan was getting back to normal.

"Tell Nasty that it's gonna get bumpy."

Milligan leaned down close to Nasty's ear and passed on the message. Weakly, Nasty raised his hand thumbs up.

"He says don't worry about him, and kick ass."

"Right," said Swanson, taking the ship down almost as steeply and directly as an elevator.

The chopper dropped right off the scopes of the pursuing force. That caused considerable consternation among them, and messages chattered back and forth. It is a fact that the larger the force, the more difficult it is to strike with surprise or precision. The flying commander saw this too late; there were too many Russian craft for them to hunt and destroy effectively. They would just get in each other's way and spend too much time wondering who was behind them, beneath them, or beside them.

The commander did the smart thing. He divided his force, sending half of them back to base. Immediately, he was countermanded.

"You will be relieved of command, Captain," barked Szymanski. In his mind, more was always better. The more choppers he had looking for the Americans, the more assured he was of finding them.

"But, sir," said the task force commander.

"Do as you're told!" snapped Szymanski.

The commander closed down his radio and swore colorfully.

Swanson was so low he was scaring himself. In the dim light the sea, a reef, a sandbar, a cluster of rocks rushed under him at immense speed. He felt as if he could almost trail his hand in the frigid water below. Any second he half expected to hear the prang and tear and then the stomach-wrenching lurch as his underbelly caught on something thrusting up from the water.

He dashed over an island, scarcely more than a set of giant rocks. It was a good sign, the first indication that real land lay somewhere up ahead. The rocks made him pull up a few feet; in so doing he drifted back on to the radar of the helicopters behind him.

"We have him on our scopes."

"Can you bring him down?"

"Not yet." The commander noted that Szymanski seemed to think that the supply of Mi-240s was unlimited. As it happened the chopper he was at the controls of was a patrol vehicle like Swanson's and just as lightly armed.

The co-pilot nudged him. Far out ahead of him, just visible in the thickening gloom, was the tail of Swanson's ship.

"We have him visually," reported the commander.

"Then kill him," said Szymanski.

"Stand by to fire." The order crackled through the fleet. "That is a command for lead ship only."

The other pilots drifted back.

The light missile that he launched was perfectly capable of blowing Swanson out of the sky. But the American-piloted craft had passed over the island now and abruptly fell to wave level again. The missiles sped past the fleeing ship and detonated deep underwater a half mile ahead. Tall geysers of foam leaped into the air.

Swanson reacted without thought. Suddenly the controls were right where he wanted them, as if he were driving his old car. He picked up speed and swung out to avoid any other projectiles that were following a path similar to the last ones.

"Spread out," yelled the Russian force commander. "There are too many of us for this circus."

He was afraid that Swanson was coming about. If the American fired into that mass there was no way he could miss hitting something. As it happened, he didn't have to.

There was an astonishing explosion as two choppers collided in mid-air and the tangled mass of machines toppled into the ocean.

Swanson heard the blast over the roar of his own engines. He dropped down and hoped for the best. Meanwhile, the Russian commander had gotten angry. He had been pushed around. He had lost a crew to treachery. He had lost two crews to incompetence. He decided that this was the extent of the losses he was going to sustain on this mission.

He fired two sets of missiles and one unerringly traced an arc directly into the fragile fuselage of Swanson's craft.

TWENTY

In a vain attempt to please his masters and serve his military pride, the force commander had selected the least lethal type of missile carried on the stubby outrigged wings of his small chopper. He had chosen the fin-stabilized type of projectile, a missile that was nothing more than a shaft of steel a foot or so long and a few inches thick. It was designed to pierce the armor of a tank, so it carried no explosive charge. It was pure steel, a large bullet, in fact, that was supposed on impact to generate immense amounts of kinetic energy that would tear its target apart. But this would happen only if it hit something hard, like a few inches of steel. The thin fabric of Swanson's chopper offered no resistance. The metal gave way and the two missiles passed through, leaving a clean wound.

In this way, the commander hoped to both shoot down the aircraft, as he dearly wanted to, and see that the escaping

men had some hope of survival, thus satisfying his order
that they be taken alive. It was the best he could do and he
hoped that he hadn't backed himself into a corner where he
would be vulnerable to military law. It was a mistaken hope,
as it turned out.

It was not as if the two shells didn't do any damage. They
did. They spiraled through the fuselage of the helicopter,
twisting and turning, gathering the guts of the craft around
the shaft of each projectile like spaghetti on a fork. There
was a crack as loud as a pistol shot fired close to the
Americans' ears as the central frame of the chopper split
against the tungsten nose of the missile. The cabin filled
with acrid electrical smoke. The engine died with an
outraged scream.

Swanson fought with the controls, trying desperately to
slow his dramatic drop toward the roiling sea. The low
altitude at which they were flying gave him nothing more
than a few precious seconds to delay his descent. The fact
that they were so low probably saved them. Even if
Swanson had had a leisurely hour to battle his stricken craft,
he couldn't have fallen from any greater height without
breaking up on impact.

He did the best he could. The helicopter hit the water
with an immense splash. Cold Arctic water cascaded into
the cockpit. Swanson was grabbing the unfamiliar buckle of
his safety harness, trying to free himself before the
helicopter either burst into flame or sank. Or both.

Milligan had never bothered to buckle himself in. The
impact of the crash had thrown him up to the ceiling and
then dumped him down in the rear of the craft, landing him
heavily on the seat where Nasty had lain. The big navigator
had also been bounced around and he was sprawled in a
lifeless heap on the floor of the copter.

The chopper rocked on the water for a second. Waves, deceptively small and low peaked from the air, crashed over the bobbing fuselage, but it stayed afloat just long enough for Swanson to throw open the door and fall into the sea.

On impact the water chilled him to the bone. A curious calm stole over him and, quite clearly, he thought, I didn't die by getting shot, I died by drowning. Then another thought occurred to him: They will never find my body.

He felt heavy and drowsy. His boots seemed suddenly to weigh hundreds of pounds. It was as if someone had suddenly attached huge weights to his feet. He could sense the bottom of the sea hundreds of fathoms below him. He wanted, just then, to go there, to let go, to allow the weight and the water to take him away from the world of death and pain and terror. It was time to give up, to surrender, not to the pursuers, but to nature, to the quiet of the inevitable.

His chin dipped into the water, then his long, dirty, unkempt hair pooled around his head. He was going now, sinking.

But the cold wouldn't let him go. If there is a power stronger than the desire to find relief through death, it is the compulsive, reflexive desire to live. Without consciously ordering his arms or legs to do anything, he felt his legs kick to drive him away from the foundering helicopter. His hands struck out, scooping back palms full of water to pull him . . . Pull him where? He swam, perhaps twenty yards, only because his body demanded it, insisted that after all the trials it had undergone he make this last, desperate struggle for life. It was the least he could do.

But he was spent. Gradually his arms made only weak token gestures at swimming. His legs continued to jerk and kick like those of the frogs he had dissected in high school, acting for no reason other than that his body felt it had to do it.

The waves rocked him soothingly, carrying him to a crest and then lowering him down into a trough, then up again. He remembered seeing the helicopter sink beneath the water, foam frothing around the rotors as the sea closed over it. He wanted to call out to Milligan, wherever he was, and say good-bye.

For some reason he felt unaccountably happy.

A swell lifted him up, but instead of sinking down again as the wave dropped, he felt himself still suspended at the height the wave had carried him to. His head knocked against something, something not hard, yet not soft, something that his wet skull bounced against. A hand was on his collar and then there was another one under his armpit. He was being hauled into a boat.

Damn, he thought, those lousy Russians. They got me after all. . . .

"No surrender," he croaked.

"Tell me about it," said Milligan, dragging his commander into the rubber life raft.

When he awoke a few minutes later, he felt as if he had been hit by a truck. He was freezing, his body felt as if it had taken a dozen or so blows from a heavyweight contender, and he had bitten his tongue painfully. For a moment he thought he had damaged his hearing. But then he knew the pounding was that of a chopper engine echoing in his ears. Then he opened his eyes and realized it wasn't one or two, but a half dozen machines circling in the darkness. They were part of the force Szymanski had assembled, and they wanted to know if there were any survivors from the helicopter so efficiently destroyed by their leader's excellent shooting.

The government man who had decided that the life raft carried aboard the patrol helicopter that now lay at the bottom of the Bering Strait was adequate for three crew members—this unknown Russian had done so secure in the knowledge that he would never have to use the raft. There was hardly room for one grown man, it was tight with two, and it could never have accommodated a third.

"Nasty," said Swanson, "he dead?"

"Yeah," said Milligan. "I mean, I guess so. He didn't move much. . . ." Milligan was curled over the edge of the dinghy, watching as the choppers crossed and recrossed an ever-widening area. It was a pretty sight. They had lights on their underbellies, lights like the ones that Milligan had so joyously blasted out of the sky just a few days before when they had all been together in their walk to freedom.

"They'll have to be awfully lucky to find us," said Milligan. "This thing isn't four feet by six and it's an awful big ocean."

Swanson watched the lights and listened to the sounds. "I wonder where the hell we are."

A wave wafted them high into the air. The two men had to shift their weight like riders on a motorcycle sidecar to keep the little craft relatively stable. With surprising gentleness the water lowered them down and rocked them in the deep trough of the wave for a second before lifting them up again.

Like a spark flying out of a fire, a chopper broke from the pack and motored out toward them. With the interest of bystanders, Milligan and Swanson watched it chatter closer. If it didn't pick them up, that was great. If it did—well, that couldn't be helped.

The light swept over the water, flashing on the wave tops, refracting off the bright white foam. The thinnest edge of the illumination, the area where the light was palest, brushed over them like a gentle wind. The chopper climbed.

"He's circling," said Milligan.

They watched the chopper spiral up into the sky and expected him to come back down for a closer look. But it didn't. It climbed to its cruising height and then turned its narrow back huffily on its fellows and chattered off into the night. When it was over a mile away, it extinguished its light abruptly and the helicopter vanished in the inky blackness.

The chopper force commander radioed Anadyr and informed Szymanski that they had downed the American helicopter in the Bering Strait and that they had seen debris floating on top of the water.

"Bodies?" demanded the man from Dzerzhinsky Square.

"Negative on that," said the force commander tersely.

"Then you must search the area until you find them. Any sign of them."

"I must break off searching now," said the chief of the flying squad. "We are low on fuel. I have already sent back three helicopters."

"Are you requesting permission, Captain?"

"No, sir, I am informing you that it is time for us to go." Otherwise, he thought, you'll have patrol craft falling into the sea like ripe apples off a tree.

"Permission granted," said Szymanski, just for the sake of appearances. Silently, he swore they would all be back the next morning at first light to continue the quest.

Wearily, the frustrated, overworked helicopters turned slowly in the night sky and headed back to their base.

Swanson and Milligan watched them go, the powerful lights going out like snuffed candles as they received the order from their leader to go home and get some rest. In a matter of minutes the sounds of the craft had faded away, leaving the two American fliers alone on the black sea.

* * *

Swanson never slept. The cold had worked itself into his wet clothes, his chilled skin, and seemingly into his heart. His exhausted body demanded sleep, but the acute discomfort of the penetrating cold refused to let him drift off. A fresh breeze was stiffening in the clear night, cooling his soaked clothing even more. Instead of sleep, his mind drifted in a strange state between wakefulness and unconsciousness, never becoming fully alert yet never sinking into the blissful oblivion of sleep.

Sometimes he thought he had passed out and was watching himself sleep. It was as if he had stepped outside of himself and was observing with bemused detachment the efforts his body was making to fight the cold, the exhaustion, to keep itself alive.

Once he had a dream of Sammy so vivid that he almost cried out, so intense was his disappointment at his waking to find it wasn't real. He had dreamed that he was getting into bed in their clean, warm bedroom. He could smell the fresh sheets; he could see his wife lying in bed, her hair spread out on the pillow like a fan. He could feel the relief as he lay down next to her and held her in his arms. . . .

But when he opened his eyes he was far from California, far from her. He was still in the rubber boat, looking at Milligan, who was staring at the sky, his eyes wide. He had such an odd look on his face. Then Swanson found himself turning colder than he was already. Frank was dead.

"Frank? Frank?"

Milligan didn't move.

"Frank!" shouted Swanson, his voice echoing across the water. "Frank!"

Milligan's eyes flicked over to his commanding officer. "What?" he said dully.

"Are you okay?"

"Yeah. I'm fine. How about you?" His voice was unnaturally calm. It worried Swanson.

"I'm fine."

"Remember what Nasty used to say?" Milligan said with sudden animation.

"What?"

Milligan was silent.

"I said, what, Frank?"

"What?" asked Milligan.

"Never mind."

"I'm so . . . thirsty," said Milligan.

Swanson figured he must have slept, because when he opened his eyes next the sky was the same lead-gray color it had been on the day before. And there was a sound. Choppers.

They were coming back. The night was over and the Russians were coming back to get them, to settle this desperate battle once and for all. They were going to take them now, after all they had gone through, after coming so close.

Swanson looked over at Milligan. The captain's eyes were shining an unnaturally bright blue in his dirty, scarred face.

"I'm sorry, Frank. We came close."

Milligan looked at him as if he no longer understood English. But something stirred in him and with a last burst of strength he pointed over the prow of the boat and said, "Look."

Swanson looked. Looming ahead of them beyond the surf was an island. A black rock pile, a windswept mass of shale and basalt that looked like a place God might have created solely for the purpose of showing that he was man's equal when it came to creating an ugly place. To Swanson it looked like paradise.

He toppled out of the boat, pulling Milligan with him. They floundered in the water for a moment, then their waterlogged, torn, and worn-out boots felt the rolling gravel of the bottom. Swanson skidded on the loose flooring, digging his heels in and trying to hold on to Milligan at the same time. The waves broke over them, but slowly they battled their way through the surf.

The choppers were louder now. The scream of engines filled their ears, and over their shoulders they could sense the menacing olive-drab bulk of two hovering craft.

The water whipped around them as they staggered ashore. Swanson dropped to his knees and rested his head on the carpet of little pebbles that made up the black beach. The walk through the water towing Milligan had done him in. He stumbled to his feet. He had to keep going; he had to get Milligan and himself to safety. He couldn't give up now. . . .

He managed another step. But the hold he had on Milligan was slipping. He tried to make his hand work, to grip the collar of Frank's flight suit, but he didn't have the strength. He slumped to the ground and clawed an inch or two forward.

The choppers still hovered somewhere above them. Swanson turned and looked back. As he did a figure, a man with a gun, walked into his line of vision and stared down at him. A round slid into the M-16 he held.

Swanson looked up at the man—he seemed to be as tall as a statue and there was something odd about him, something Swanson found unbelievably strange. He wanted to ask Frank if he saw it as well. Then it hit him. The man was black skinned and he was wearing a set of fatigues with the anchor-and-globe badge of the U.S. Marine Corps.

Swanson opened his mouth to say something, but the leatherneck beat him to the punch.

"You say a word," said the man, "you move a muscle, man, and you'll just be another dead Russian on my beach."

LEWIS PERDUE

THE TESLA BEQUEST
A secret society of powerful men have stolen the late Nikola Tesla's plans for a doomsday weapon; they are just one step away from ruling the world.
☐ 42027-7 THE TESLA BEQUEST $3.50

THE DELPHI BETRAYAL
From the depths of a small, windowless room in the bowels of the White House, an awesome conspiracy to create economic chaos and bring the entire world to its knees is unleashed.
☐ 41728-4 THE DELPHI BETRAYAL $2.95

QUEENS GATE RECKONING
A wounded CIA operative and a defecting Soviet ballerina hurtle toward the hour of reckoning as they race the clock to circumvent twin assassinations that will explode the balance of power.
☐ 41436-6 QUEENS GATE RECKONING $3.50

THE DA VINCI LEGACY
A famous Da Vinci whiz, Curtis Davis, tries to uncover the truth behind the missing pages of an ancient manuscript which could tip the balance of world power toward whoever possesses it.
☐ 41762-4 THE DA VINCI LEGACY $3.50

ALLEN DRURY

"Drury is a slick writer and knows the ingredients that go into the making of a bestseller."
—West Coast Review of Books

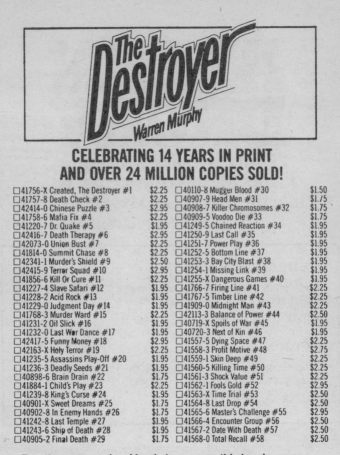